LEAVING THE BELLWEATHERS

KRISTIN CLARK VENUTI

EGMONT
USA

NEW YORK

EGMONT
We bring stories to life

First published by Egmont USA, 2009
443 Park Avenue South, Suite 806
New York, NY 10016

1 3 5 7 9 8 6 4 2

WWW.EGMONTUSA.COM
WWW.LEAVINGTHEBELLWEATHERS.COM

Library of Congress Cataloging-in-Publication Data

Venuti, Kristin Clark.
Leaving the Bellweathers / Kristin Clark Venuti.
p.   cm.
Summary: In Eel-Smack-by-the-Bay, put-upon butler Tristan Benway
writes a memoir of his years spent working for the chaotic and
eccentric Bellweather family in their lighthouse as he prepares for his
long-awaited departure from indentured servitude.
ISBN 978-1-60684-006-1 (hardcover)
ISBN 978-1-60684-050-4 (reinforced library binding)
[1. Household employees—Fiction. 2. Eccentrics and eccentricities—Fiction.
3. Family life—Fiction. 4. Authorship—Fiction. 5. Lighthouses—Fiction.
6. Humorous stories.] I. Title.
PZ7.V57Le 2009 [Fic]—dc22 2009016244

Book design by Lizzy Bromley

Printed in the United States of America

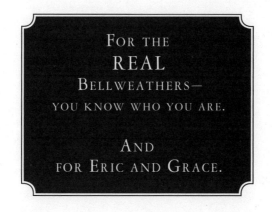

FOR THE
REAL
BELLWEATHERS—
YOU KNOW WHO YOU ARE.

AND
FOR ERIC AND GRACE.

CONTENTS

LEAVING THE BELLWEATHERS

The Sad Story of Myself,
Benway,
As Told by Myself
(mostly)
Regarding the
Misadventures of the
Family Bellweather
and the Man
who Cleaned Up
after Them

By
Tristan Benway

I t is nighttime in the village of Eel-Smack-by-the-Bay. All is quiet except for the chirp of crickets and the occasional moist ribbit of a bullfrog. A slanted yellow patch of lamplight shines through a window and rests softly on the grass. Certainly there is nothing in this peaceful scene to hint that pandemonium is likely to break out at any moment. On the third floor of the Lighthouse on the Hill, an upright man sits in an upright chair, at an upright desk, up writing in his diary.

The Journal of T. Benway

Introduction
Why I Am Here and Should Not Be

July 7,
Glorious Liberation and Oath Abandonment
Time (GLOAT) minus 8 weeks, 2 hours, and 27
minutes

For many years now, I have served the family
Bellweather in my loyal, dedicated, and hardworking fashion. Indeed, they are the only
employers I have ever had. Old William
Bellweather (a fine if slightly eccentric gent)
hired me upon my graduation from the very
prestigious B. Knighted Academy for Butlers.
The fact that he hired me directly from the
academy had nothing to do with my stellar
credentials (despite my natural modesty, I must
mention here that I did graduate first in my
class). No, his reason for hiring me was due to a

circumstance beyond the control of either of us.

Come September the First (a mere 8 weeks, 2 hours, and 26 minutes from now) it will have been 200 hundred years and 14 days since Horatio Bellweather stood on deck as the <u>HMS Scurvy</u> set sail for the new world. On the sixth day of the voyage, there was a terrible storm, the ship was wrecked, and Horatio Bellweather (who in true eccentric Bellweather fashion never traveled anywhere without his grandfather clock) saved Nigel Benway, by allowing him to share his perch on the large, wooden timepiece. Eight days later, when they reached dry land, my great-great-great-great-grandfather pledged to serve Horatio Bellweather. Of course, this was merely a formality, since he had been indentured to the man for two years already. ("Indentured" is a polite way of saying that he was little more than a slave.) Evidently my forebear felt a grander gesture was needed, and so he pledged the loyalty and service of his descendants for the next two hundred years.

I am not trying to be witty when I say that this oath was surely going overboard.

The wretched terms of "The Benway Family Oath of Fealty"—on parchment in a fine, upright hand—have been passed on from generation to generation. The document itself—hidden away in a safe and secure, if dusty, place—reads thus:

BENWAY FAMILY OATH OF FEALTY

I, NIGEL BENWAY,

being of
EXTREMELY GRATEFUL
mind and body, not to mention
MOST EXCELLENT PENMANSHIP—
no Small Feat for an Indentured Servant,
if I say so Myself—

do hereby pledge my life to the Service of

HORATIO BELLWEATHER
AND HIS DESCENDANTS

in return for that individual's

Selfless and Heroic Act of

SAVING ME FROM THE

FATE OF DROWNING.

As I would be Very Unlikely to have

any Progeny had I drowned, it is Fitting

and Right that I should hereby

Pledge the Loyalty and Service
of My Descendants to

THE BELLWEATHER FAMILY
for the next

TWO HUNDRED YEARS.

———— ✦ ————

Signed,

(With the aforementioned

Most Excellent Penmanship)

Nigel Benway

As I am the Last of the Line and an orphan, the information regarding my fine family and their Wretched Oath of Fealty was impressed upon me from the earliest age by the Headmaster at the B. Knighted Academy for Butlers, where I was raised. I have always taken great pride in the Benway Family Honor of Keeping the Oath.

The happy news is that the two hundred years are nearly up, and I will be free of this circus which masquerades as a household. You see, Dear Journal, when Old William Bellweather passed on, I continued in the service of his son, the famous inventor Eugene Bellweather, PhD. For the past several years, I have tended to the domestic affairs of the most chaotic family ever to live.

In a lighthouse.

It is no easy task to run a household in a lighthouse.

A circular staircase winds up through the middle of the building from the basement lair to the observation deck. Seven floors of semicircular-shaped rooms surround this staircase. This means that should the triplets, in their seventh-floor art studio (more about them later), leave a mess for someone else to clean up (that someone else being Your Most Humble Servant, of course), the necessary mops, sponges, forklifts, and what-have-you must be retrieved from their place of storage on the second floor and carried up exactly one hundred and forty-two steps. Oh yes, Your Most Humble Servant has counted those steps.

Often.

One would think that a man with Eugene Bellweather's mighty reputation for invention could come up with a device to spare the legs of his faithful family retainer. . . .

Indeed, I have lived under circumstances and through events beyond imagination.

And so, I set down here in the third person, as though someone else were telling the tale (my lot is much easier to bear this way in that I may pretend that these events happened to someone other than me), a litany of What I Have Suffered. That which follows is my* account of the Bellweathers' activities of a single summer. As fantastic as it sounds, it is all true.

*Oh, all right! A very few Minor and Inconsequential Details have been filled in by certain other members of the family.

A REMOVABLE FEAST

An unusual meal in the household Bellweather would be a quiet affair. With murmured "please"es and "thank you"s, the family would pass the delicious dishes that Benway placed before them. Perhaps they would go around the table and tell one another mildly amusing stories about the various things they had encountered in the course of the day.

Tonight's meal was, alas, more typical.

It began with thirteen-year-old Ninda Bellweather dragging a bewildered-looking guest into the dining room.

"Every one, this is Mr. Miller," she introduced, indicating the man who shuffled his feet before them. He was the very picture of a storybook hobo, if there is such a thing. He held a red-tied bandana, which presumably carried all his worldly possessions, and on his feet were worn-out boots, one of which had come apart at the sole so that his toes stuck out.

"Uh, Dusty," the guest corrected, his voice gravelly and uncertain. "Dusty Miller. I'm much obliged . . ."

"He's been oppressed," Ninda interrupted. "We're going to feed him dinner."

"Well, now . . . I do appreciate that . . . ," Dusty Miller said, sniffing the air. If he hoped to get a whiff of the mouthwatering meal Ninda had promised him, he was surely disappointed. The most pervasive smell in the Lighthouse on the Hill is always that of fresh paint.

The Bellweather children's mother, Lillian, and nine-year-old triplets, Spike, Brick, and Sassy, were already seated at the curved dining room table. Fourteen-year-old Spider was fussing with a cage containing either a very angry cat or an orange demon.

He bent a small piece of wire around the latch.

"That ought to hold," he said, giving the howling enclosure a pat and then taking a seat.

Spider is a lover of endangered animals . . . but only the sort who have the ability to poison, maim, or kill people.

The animal in the cage was not endangered, however. Spider's interest was due to local lore. The orange tom's neighborhood nickname was "Thunder Paw" and the small beast was said to have beaten two Great Danes and one Dalmatian into submission. Spider wished to study this fearsome happening and had plans to release the animal after dark (he himself never went out in the daylight if it could be helped) so that he could track it.

Thunder Paw was not taking kindly to his confinement. He screeched and hissed and made altogether terrible sounds. The rest of the family took no more notice of this than they had of Dusty Miller, who took a hasty step backward, bumping into a wall. A vibrant, purplish paint smeared across his back and down the right sleeve of his ragged jacket.

He turned his arm this way and that, inspecting the damage.

"Oh, dear!" Mrs. Bellweather said, taking her dreamy blue eyes off what had been the freshly painted wall's periwinkle perfection and noticing the unfamiliar person in their midst.

"Er, don't worry, ma'am," Dusty Miller said. He clearly didn't realize that visitors to the Lighthouse on the Hill usually came away with wide swaths of paint decorating their garments. "It'll wash."

Mrs. Bellweather's eyes came all the way into focus. "I expect it will—but I'll just wait until it dries and touch it up then. No sense in washing recently painted walls." She bobbed her titian curls in Dusty Miller's direction, acknowledging his gallant concern for her beautiful walls.

Lillian Bellweather is a painter. What she paints are the inside walls of the Lighthouse on the Hill.

She Never Stops.

Nary has a room in the Bellweather home escaped the frequent caress of her brush.

"You know," said Mrs. Bellweather in her genuine,

sweet voice, "I do believe that wet walls are teaching the children good posture." She laughed in a silvery, bell-like way. "Perhaps these lessons could benefit you as well."

Dusty Miller closed his open mouth. It never occurred to anyone to argue with Mrs. Bellweather. It would be like arguing with a rainbow—or a brilliant sunset. It was just far nicer to look at her. Even her argumentative husband felt this way, and it was generally agreed among the rest of the family that Dr. Bellweather would argue with a stone if the mood so struck him.

Ninda nudged her still-staring guest into a vacant chair and sat down beside him. Spike was seated to his left, holding a pair of hedgerow clippers. The vagrant felt a tug at the bottom of his coat. He looked down to discover that Spike had snipped a large hole in it.

Dusty glanced over at Mrs. Bellweather to see her reaction to her child's misdeed. There was none. She was focused on her walls again.

"W-why in the world did you do that?" he sputtered at Spike.

"I'M MAKING ART!!!!" Spike wasn't upset in the least. He shouted his explanation because it is an unfortunate fact that the triplets never communicate at a decibel below earsplitting unless they are Up to No Good. Then they whisper. When that happens, hairs on the necks of animals and humans alike stand on end, for near-disaster always follows in the wake of that terrible sound.

No one at the table reacted to Spike's extraordinary statement. Dusty tried to digest this as another snarling added itself to the yowls of the outraged feline. The hobo looked toward the doorway, apprehension on his face. He could hear shouting that was getting closer.

"This is the third time this week you have ruined my concentration! I may never invent another thing at this rate . . . and if I don't, you know what will happen, Benway, don't you?"

Professor Eugene Bellweather charged into the dining room, his eyebrows fairly leaping. The doctor is the very picture of a mad scientist and possessed of very *busy* eyebrows that wiggle and jump and draw themselves together in a scowl. When he's enraged, they shake so much that, upon occasion, witnesses have expressed fear that they might fall right off his face.

The professor's eyebrows usually go through some warm-ups before they start their calisthenics. This must have happened while he traversed the stairs from his fifth-floor lab to the dining room, for his eyebrows were frenzied by the time he seated himself at the table. He continued his tirade, heeding neither the rattling, howling cage just behind Sassy's chair, nor the stranger seated between Ninda and Spike.

Benway ignored the shouting and simply began putting food on the table. He placed the heavier items, such as the soup tureen, just out of Dr. Bellweather's reach, for the professor had a tendency to throw things.

A large roast beef was placed just in front of Ninda's guest, whose expression contained a peculiar and growing mix of apprehension, bewilderment, and greed.

The family has always insisted that Dr. Bellweather's stomping and shouting and throwing things are mere demonstrations of his outlandish sense of humor, and they take no more notice of these than they do any of the bizarre things that happen in the Lighthouse on the Hill. It was understandably harrowing to one not used to it, however.

"I won't be able to afford your wages, Benway!" Dr. Bellweather shouted. "That's what will happen. I'll have no money to keep body and soul together! We'll lose the house! My children will be forced to work in an airless, dark factory somewhere!"

Dusty Miller shrank back in his seat, clearly hoping to escape the notice of this deranged man.

Ninda was outraged . . . but not for the reason you may suppose.

"Oh, ho! So airless, dark factory rooms are fine for the masses of humanity enslaved in them, but not for *your* children! Don't you think that the people who are forced to work in such places have families? What makes *your* family so special?" Her clear blue eyes darkened and narrowed as they always did when she perceived an injustice.

"US!" screamed the nine-year-old triplets, answering

Ninda's question. "WE MAKE IT SPECIAL!" added Sassy, the girl, pulling out a jar of honey and standing on her chair.

From her teetering position she reached across the table to glub honey onto the triplets' mashed turnips. The howling from the cage behind her finally registered.

"OH, MRS. NORRIS CALLED A LITTLE WHILE AGO," she shouted at Spider.

He looked up quickly. "What did she say?" he asked.

"SHE WANTED TO KNOW IF WE'D SEEN HER CAT," Sassy shrieked, jerking her head back to indicate the confined beast behind her. It is an unfortunate thing that the movement was not more subtle, because it caused her to lose her balance.

Chair and child crashed backward, hitting the cage, which sprang open, releasing a cat possessed with all the fury of Hades.

Sassy was unhurt. The triplets have a reputation for being indestructible. The beast shot across the table, and Dusty Miller had a brief but painful view of two Thunderous Paws as they smacked his face.

The monster clawed to the top of his head and then leaped off to streak around the room. Sassy scrambled after the animal, heedless of place settings and soup tureens. Spike and Brick dove across the table knocking over platters and glasses. (Why should Sassy have all the fun?)

The cat yowled, the professor shouted, the triplets shrieked, the dishes broke, and the walls were smeared.

When it was over, an orange-and-periwinkle cat with thunderous paws had escaped through the open window like a meteor. Dusty Miller and the roast beef had disappeared forever as well.

Typical.

———————>•<———————

July 8,
GLOAT minus 7 weeks, 6 days, 4 hours, and 17 minutes

Dear Journal,
Ninda brought home another of her "guests"

today. He left rather abruptly. I, for one, was glad to see him go—even if that did mean a vegetarian meal for the Bellweathers. Had he stayed, I'd have had to shoo him out of my bed, no doubt. Ninda frequently offers the use of my living quarters to those she feels to be Downtrodden by Society. . . . I don't know which I mind more, really: her tendency to do that, or her excessively loud bagpipe playing.

On the other hand, Ninda has been instrumental in helping me find a way to fund my retirement. Imagine my dismay not long ago, upon discovering that reversals in the stock market had turned my tidy little nest egg into a tiny little nest egg, and that I now lacked the means to support myself after the Glorious Day of my Liberation 7 weeks, 6 days, 4 hours, and 15 minutes from now.

I do not wish this family ill; however, I shall publish my account of them. I believe literature of this sort is called "tell-all." You see, Dr. Bellweather and his family have always been of interest to those in the outside world. I believe this is partly due to the professor's reputation for invention and partly due to his outlandish fits.

Lest my plan seem disloyal, let me hasten to point out that the idea itself was proposed by a member of the family.

Ninda had come to my quarters, as she occasionally does, to inquire if I was feeling Downtrodden or Exploited. At some point she said, and I quote, "Benway, the things you put up with could fill a book." While not explicit, I believe that permission for the project was Certainly Implied.

Who better to tell the Bellweathers' story than their household servant? Better still, one who has been logging their activities already? I do not understand the Bellweathers (indeed, who could?); however, as family butler, I posses much information that is unavailable to anyone else, and I am certainly capable of passing it along. After all, I have been forced to observe their shenanigans up close.

A good servant quietly watches all that goes on in an establishment, in order to better meet the needs of that household's members. A great servant uses discreetly placed spy cameras.

I have been a great servant for some time now. (Such methods are used purely in the interests of self-preservation considering the dangerous nature of this family's activities . . . not because I am a household snoop, as some may be tempted to infer!)

When the manuscript is published, I will have enough money to retire. I will, of course, have to change my name from Tristan Benway to something like John Smyth. Also, the locale to which I move shall Definitely have to be Far, Far Away.

This suits me for a couple of different reasons. The first, of course, is the notion of the peace I shall have when I am no longer subjected to the outrageous antics of this family. Second, and more importantly, Dr. Bellweather has assured me that he will do something unpleasant to me, possibly involving a corkscrew and the soft tissue of my skin, should I ever expose the details of his family's adventures. The family might say that this is simply another of his little jokes. . . . Still Far, Far Away will suit me well, and so I make a solemn vow. Just as surely as my ancestor pledged to serve the Bellweather family, I do hereby Pledge to Leave them the very day that the Wretched Benway Family Oath of Fealty is fulfilled— 7 weeks, 6 days, 4 hours, and 12 minutes from now.

SPIDER AND
THE DOGCATCHER

The day was the lovely sort of early summer day that most consider perfect for picnicking, hiking, or even sailing. Spider Bellweather considered it perfect for sitting in his basement bedroom, bathed in the gloomy half-light of any one of the fourteen computers he had refurbished. These were set up on the very long wooden table that lined one wall of his room.

He took a break from hacking to visit his favorite Website—www.Endangeredspecieshavingtheability tomaimorkillinagruesomemanner.com—and up popped one of the most horrifying pictures he had ever had the joy to gaze upon.

In the photograph, a stark white alligator possessed of red eyes grinned at the camera in a most evil manner. A single, high-top tennis shoe protruded from its mouth. Underneath the photo there appeared a short article about the plight of the Endangered Albino Alligator, along with a headline that read, "Won't You Help?"

The Albino Alligator (gatorodylus acutus blancus, *subphylum* vertebrata) *of South America needs your help. This rare and dangerous animal's survival is threatened by encroaching development of its habitat, as well as the fact that they are easy targets for poachers. Despite their documented viciousness toward other creatures, these alligators are the only reptiles known to care for their young once hatched. Only twenty-two of the grand, vicious beasts remain on the planet. Knowledgeable herpetologists are asked to open their hearts and homes to these endangered monsters. GAGA*

(Grand Albino Gators Anonymous) requests that interested parties donate money to the foundation to cover the cost of shipping.

Spider pushed his chair back from the computer and climbed into the hammock, which was strung from wall to curved wall in his bedroom.

Spider's lair suits him well. The windows of his dank and musty chamber are few and high, letting in very little light. He was quite pleased when his mother painted the room black, less so when she returned the following week and repainted it burnt sienna. Spider retreats to his hammock to do his Deepest Thinking. The family knows never to disturb Spider in his Deep Thought sessions. Even Benway defers to them, leaving the lair and coming back to clean it only when Spider is obviously no longer thus engaged.

Among the things Spider likes to Think Deeply about are ways to help endangered species. But only those which have the ability to poison, maim, or kill people. He feels these creatures to be misunderstood by society. His dearest ambition in life has always been to open up an animal reserve for them.

The family will be grateful when that happens, because that means he will no longer be bringing such beasts into the Bellweather home.

Spider lay back and closed his eyes. Just last week Thaddeus Bohack, head of the Eel-Smack-by-the-Bay Department of Animal Control, had caught up with Spider outside the exotic pet food market. Spider was warned that were he to harbor vicious beasts ever again, he would be sent away to the St. Whiplash Academy for Rebellious Boys. The incident that resulted in this threat had been a small one, really, but it *had* involved the Mayor of Eel-Smack's poodle and a band of vicious spotted wallabies brought to Eel-Smack by Spider himself.

Thus threatened, Spider had concluded that his plans for a wild animal reserve would have to wait until he was too old to be sent to the academy. He pushed off the wall with his foot, setting the hammock in lazy motion. That decision to wait had been made *before* he discovered the plight of the Albino Alligators, though.

This endangered animal that had the ability to maim or kill *needed* him. Was he one of those hypocrites who placed his own comfort (and freedom) above the survival of an entire species? Besides, the Lighthouse on the Hill was firmly on land, so if he kept the reserve there, he couldn't really be said to be *harboring* the beasts, could he? Harboring implied water, he was sure of it.

To be on the safe side, he would start small—perhaps with just one Endangered Albino Alligator . . . and surely *one* Endangered Albino Alligator would not be enough to attract the attention of Thaddeus Bohack. Certainly he, Spider, would take excellent care of the poor beast—and Benway would clean up after it, so that there would be no evidence of its existence in the Lighthouse on the Hill whatsoever. It would all be very discreet.

Feeling clever, he crept out of the hammock and prepared to leave his lair.

Spider rarely ventures from the basement when the sun is out, but when he must, he dons a hat to cover the curly blond hair that tends to straggle into his face. He puts on aviator sunglasses to protect his used-to-the-dim-light-of-the-lair eyes, and he covers himself in Eugene Bellweather's cast-off trench coat in order to preserve his pallor.

Besides helping him to avoid the sun, he believes this getup lends him an air of mystery which he finds entirely to his liking. Not that he would ever in a million geologic years admit that he cared what sort of impression he made on the good villagers of Eel-Smack-by-the-Bay—and in particular on one villager who just happened to work at the exotic pet food market and who just happened to sport a beatific smile and wavy, black, raven's-wing hair.

Just as Spider reached the top of the basement stairs, the foghorn blared. The doorbell in the Lighthouse on the Hill is connected to it. It is extremely loud. The worst part, though, is that it disturbs Dr. Bellweather's concentration. When that happens, he flings open the window of his fifth-floor laboratory and throws things down at hapless individuals whose only crime has been to ring a doorbell. The professor refuses to disconnect the horn, despite repeated requests that he do so. One can only assume that this little game appeals to his bizarre sense of humor.

The person on the front porch had obviously visited the Bellweather home before. He stood with his body pressed tightly against the lighthouse to avoid being hit on the head. When Spider opened the door, the visitor pitched into the front hall. The phrase "Speak of the devil" came to Spider's mind, because there, stumbling into the Lighthouse on the Hill, was Thaddeus Bohack.

The head of Animal Control is a gaunt man with a sharply hooked nose that forever seems to be sniffing around for trouble. Fortunately, he always wears a pith helmet. This makes him recognizable from such a distance that Spider is usually able to avoid him.

The dogcatcher (for that's what he is, despite the fancy title) glared at Spider as though losing his balance was somehow the boy's fault.

"Good afternoon, sir," Spider said. He peered up the circular staircase, hoping to spot Benway. He was aware that Benway's dignified demeanor was held a little in awe by the villagers, including Bohack. Spider was not above using Benway to shield himself from verbal assault.

"I had a missing-cat report today—what do you know about it?" the man demanded.

"Nothing at all, *sir.*" Spider emphasized the last word, taking care to be especially polite in the obvious absence of Benway.

"You haven't imported any more spotted wallabies have you?" Bohack's hooked nose quivered.

"No, sir," Spider answered.

"No pointy-eared Tasmanian devils?"

"No, sir."

"No razor-toothed giraffes?"

"No, sir."

"No cat-eating tortoises?"

"No, s–" Spider interrupted himself, excited. "There is such an animal?!"

The dogcatcher did not take Spider's sudden interest well at all.

"I don't know!" he thundered at the boy. "But if

there is, and one shows up in Eel-Smack-by-the-Bay, I'll have you in St. Whiplash's so fast you won't have time to pack a toothbrush! Understand?!"

Spider nodded his head.

Bohack adjusted his pith helmet.

"I'm watching you, Spider. Just remember that," he snarled before storming back out of the Lighthouse on the Hill.

Spider waited a moment, until he was quite sure the nasty fellow was on his way down the hill. Then, brushing aside the slight unease that quite naturally comes to one who has been threatened with a stint at a reform school, he went off to find his mother in the scarlet room. She was painting it a light, eggshell blue.

"May I use your credit card to pay for importing an endangered brute that might maim or kill us, please?" He had to shout to be heard over the sound of the bagpipes Ninda was practicing upstairs.

"Why, certainly," his mother said, shouting as well.

It was *so* nice to have a mother who believed in encouraging her children's little schemes and hobbies.

July 11,
GLOAT minus 7 weeks, 3 days, 2 hours, and 42 minutes

Dear Journal,

Endangered Albino Alligator indeed! I cannot understand the notion of allowing such a beast to roam loose in the Lighthouse on the Hill. Spider will never consent to caging the animal, but I've no doubt that he will certainly assume that I shall clean up after it!

The monster will make messes on the furniture and snap at people. Hmmm . . . of course, I shouldn't like to see the triplets badly hurt, but a little snapping . . . well, that doesn't seem so harmful, now does it?

I am forced to consider not only the prospect of discomfort but issues of safety as well. No man in his right mind would consent to remain in the employ of these madhouse inmates indefinitely.

Of course, in this Enlightened and Modern Age, it would be a Difficult Thing to force a man to remain in servitude because of a two-hundred-year-old oath. I am not just any man, I am a Benway.

We Benways have always been Men of Honor. An Oath of Fealty, no matter how Wretched or Ludicrous one knows it to be, is an Oath of Fealty. I may not be of the mind that Benways are rightly destined to serve—but I do believe that Benways must keep their word.

I am quite hopeful that my method of self-support in retirement will smooth my path. I gathered together several pages from my journal and sent them to a good friend who is Well Placed in the publishing industry. He is most enthusiastic about the project and believes he can help me.

In exactly 7 weeks, 3 days, 2 hours, and 39 minutes, when the terms of that Wretched Oath of Fealty are up, I shall Go Away! Indeed, I have already sent for a Real Estate guide to Charming

Cottages in Warm Locales Far, Far Away. We'll just see how this family manages without me!

Or perhaps I won't see, since as I've said, I have vowed to go Far, Far Away from them.

· 3 ·
THE TROUBLES OF POSTMAN GRIMSBY

In the week that followed, Spider busied himself reading everything he could about establishing an Endangered Animal Reserve. He realized that it was not enough to save one Endangered Albino Alligator. Once he had settled this first one in, he would see about sending for additional beasts.

He began to hang around the mailbox, setting up an outdoor office by dragging his laptop computer, a desk, and a small bookcase out into the yard. His mother put down her paintbrush long enough to go out and take a picture of this, as it was the first time in many years that Spider had been observed in the front yard during daylight hours.

He stuffed four pounds of hamburger meat into an ice chest as a treat for the gator when it arrived and passed the time by memorizing complex algebraic problems. He practiced speaking Japanese with a French accent. He practiced speaking French with a Japanese accent.

For their part, the triplets thoughtfully entertained him by pruning part of the hedgerow into a topiary. The clipped shrubbery now depicts two of Spider's heroes, Darwin and Galileo, arm wrestling.

The outdoor nature of this project led to an interest in a different art form, which the triplets gleefully called "Environmental Art with a Living Element." This meant that the three dug traps for the postman, Mr. Grimsby, to fall into.

Every day Grimsby picked his way carefully across the yard to the mailbox, taking care not to fall into the traps. After the first two times it happened, the mailman had become alert to that particular danger.

Spider took to phoning Animal Control and using

a disguised voice to report packs of wild dogs and colonies of wild kangaroos that were supposedly running amok on the other side of Eel-Smack. This kept Bohack busy and far away from the Lighthouse on the Hill when the mail was due to arrive.

And so it was that several days into Spider's wait (just when he was in danger of losing his pallor) the dogcatcher was nowhere around when a stone-faced Grimsby drove a large mail truck up the hill.

Grimsby parked. He got out, clomped around to the back of the truck, slid a door up, pulled a ramp down, and disappeared into it. He emerged pushing a huge wooden box down the ramp on a dolly. Spider grabbed the small ice chest of hamburger (which was by now quite rancid) and sprinted across the yard, avoiding the triplets' traps.

Generally, large crates that came to the Bellweathers' house contained objects both amazing and fantastic. Sometimes, before Benway could stop him, Grimsby even put on a bit of a show of opening whatever it was right out on the front lawn. "Got to make sure it got here in good condition, heh, heh."

This crate, however, was a different matter. For one thing, it was plastered all over with warnings and cautions. (This naturally thrilled Spider.) For another, it emitted a rather swampy smell. And finally, there were the rustling and snapping sounds that came from within.

"Well, there you are," Grimsby said, backing toward his truck. "Heh, heh. I'll just be on my way, then. Got a lot of mail left to deliver." Still backing away. "Gonna leave you to it. Course, you got that lot to help you," he said, defending himself by indicating the excited triplets and Ninda, who had come up from the beach to watch.

Spider examined the crate closely. "Looks like they've used an extraordinary number of nails," he observed with satisfaction. "I'll need a crowbar, Grimsby. Is there one in the truck?" he asked.

"Well, now that you ask . . . heh, heh . . . not a one," Grimsby said, putting more distance between his body and the rustly, snappy, swampy box.

"Nonsense. Would you fetch it for me?" Spider asked, in a tone that commanded rather than inquired.

He put down the cooler and wiped his hands on the grass.

Grimsby sighed and got the crowbar.

He handed it to the boy, then stood back, arms folded across his chest. In a burst of maternal-ish feeling, Ninda put a reassuring arm around her little sister's shoulder. This was shaken off when Sassy stepped in to get a closer view.

Spider wedged the end of the bar into a slight crack along the edge of the box and pried. A small piece of wood broke off. Spider tried again, bearing down on the crowbar with all of his might. Another small piece broke off.

"You're doin' fine," Grimsby said. "That's it, put your back into it," he encouraged Spider from the other side of the mail truck. Spider tried again, to no avail.

Finally Grimsby was forced to take the crowbar and pry the thing open himself. He seemed nervous, and would have been more so had he noticed Spider hanging back and readying himself with fistfuls of hamburger meat. The postman pried one of the narrow boards off the top. From underneath the crack of the breaking wood, there was again that unnerving rustling and snapping. Taking a deep breath, he wedged the crowbar into the narrow space and pushed. The two sides of the crate split open, and the great, white brute was revealed. The distance from its snout to its tail was easily that of a cub scout and a half. The beast swung his massive head around toward Grimsby. The postman jumped back when the beady, red eyes narrowed with what looked like menace. Into the momentarily stunned silence came the sound of alligator teeth snapping.

"No sudden moves," Spider called out, too late. Grimsby had already started to run. Now everyone knows that one should *never* run from an Endangered Albino Alligator. They consider this a challenge and are likely to pursue their prey. It is unfortunate indeed that Grimsby was possibly the only person in the world who did not know this.

Grimsby had a head start, but Albino Alligators are notoriously fast, and this one, jaws chomping, had almost caught up with him when the postman fell into one of the triplet's deeper pits. The animal was clearly irritated by this turn of events. The trap was narrow but surprisingly deep, considering that it was the work of three nine-year-olds, and he could see no way to get at Grimsby.

The beast circled the pit, regarding Grimsby through his blood-red eyes and snapping his teeth together every few seconds.

"QUICK, SOMEONE! CALL THE POLICE," Sassy shouted.

"CALL AN AMBULANCE," Brick yelled.

"CALL THE MORGUE," shrieked Spike.

"No need for any of that." Spider's voice carried with it such authority that all fell silent.

"Hey, boy," Spider called to get the attention of the alligator. He then lobbed a fistful of hamburger, which landed not far from the alligator's snout. The gator sniffed, and then gobbled it, looking for all the world like a dog that's been given a treat. He then returned to clacking his teeth at Grimsby, who cowered in the deep recess of the pit. "Hey, boy," Spider called, again grabbing a fistful of meat from the cooler and throwing it. This time the gator didn't sniff it; he just gobbled, and then hesitated for an instant before turning back toward Grimsby. Spider threw more of the hamburger, this time a little distance from the pit but within the animal's line of sight. Slowly the beast moved toward the meat. He ate it, turned, and gave one halfhearted snap before looking up at Spider.

And so they advanced toward the lighthouse, Spider calling, "Hey, boy," and tossing balls of meat, the alligator eating them. When they got close to the porch steps, Spider ran out of meat. He held the cooler open to show the gator there was nothing inside. The others gasped when the alligator charged Spider. The animal knocked the cooler out of Spider's hand then nosed it around on the ground for a minute, as if he needed to see for himself that there wasn't any food left. Satisfied that this was the case, he advanced on Spider once again. Spider stood still, honoring the simple rule that everyone knows: You must never, ever run from an Endangered Albino Alligator. When the gator reached Spider, he stopped and butted his snout against Spider's leg. Spider leaned over and rubbed the brute's head just as you would scratch a dog behind the ears. The beast closed his eyes in ecstasy. Spider smiled down at him.

"Hey, boy," Spider spoke soothingly as he scratched. "How about if I call you 'Heyboy'?" The gator rubbed against Spider's shins, as though he approved of his name. Spider carefully led Heyboy up the steps and into his new home, the Lighthouse on the Hill.

You shall have to wait and see for yourself how the boy managed to establish the first-ever Endangered Albino Alligator Habitat, but what happened to the postman can be revealed here in two sentences.

Ninda had one heck of a time talking him out of the pit. Mail service to the Lighthouse on the Hill never did resume.

———⟫●⟪———

July 18,
GLOAT minus 6 weeks, 3 days, 3 hours, and 12 minutes

Dear Journal,

What calamity! New duties include walking to the post office to collect the daily mail. I simply cannot understand the thrill the children seem to be getting from the arrival of Heyboy. Alas, this is just the tip of the iceberg, as they say.

The Grimsby traps have ushered in a "digging phase" of the triplets' so-called art creation. The once-lovely garden resembles nothing so much as a Hollywood movie set for a film about the devastating battlefields of war.

My zinnias exist only in memory—indeed only in _my_ memory, it seems. No one but Mrs. Bellweather has taken notice of my distress—though her response to the situation is one that is Unsatisfying to me.

"Oh, but it's beautiful and symbolic that the little dears should be creating art in the earth," she cooed before turning back to her art—the walls of the upstairs lavatory.

Her statement begs the question, symbolic of what? Being Supremely and Elegantly

Professional, I of course did not argue with her. (Not that anyone ever does.) I instead soothed myself with visions of the tropical garden I will plant in 6 weeks, 3 days, 3 hours, and 10 minutes. Indeed, being a forward-looking chap, I've already sent for tropical seeds for the garden I intend to plant when I retire to my own Charming Cottage in a Warm Location Far, Far Away.

Nevertheless, I am resolved to encourage the "little dears" to explore a different medium.* Not that they will listen to me. Indeed I might as well be a zinnia myself for all the influence I hold over this family.

As for the likelihood of the Bellweathers managing to locate a butler who would be willing to replace me in this combination madhouse and zoo . . . Good Luck to Them, I say. Not that it will occur to them to miss <u>me</u>—really anyone who cleans their messes and serves their meals will do.

---

*Editorial Note: My Noble Sense of Honesty later forced me to admit that the effect of my encouragement of the triplets in their Exploration of Other Artistic Avenues was disastrous—and very nearly caused an International Incident.

This matters not one whit—at the B. Knighted Academy for Butlers, we were trained to maintain a certain professional distance. Their affection (or lack thereof) is of no consequence to me, I'm sure. It is my duty to see to their needs—and that is all.

I simply believe it will be Very Difficult for them to attract competent household help. I attended school with some very fine fellows, despite the fact that they did not graduate first in their class (there could only be one of us, and I believe I may have mentioned that I had that honor). Those chaps would never put up with the things I have had to due to the Wretched Benway Family Oath of Fealty.

Still, Wretched Oath or No—I am not without a sense of my duty toward this family—and so I shall set myself about the task of advertising for, interviewing, and hiring my own replacement.

·4·
THE PROFESSOR VS. NINDA

Within a surprisingly short time, the family grew accustomed to having Heyboy in the house. He was a remarkably docile creature who only ever seemed to snap at the professor and Benway. The others took this as a sign of Heyboy's intelligence.

"AFTER ALL, THEY'RE THE ONLY TWO WHO DON'T WANT HIM IN THE HOUSE!" Sassy shrieked to Spike and Brick over the flower bed they were digging up. Benway had hinted to them that Environmental Art was becoming overdone, but until they could come up with a different medium—hopefully one which would cause the world to Sit Up and Take Notice—they continued with the digging. For the present, they simply renamed it Experimenting with Negative Space.

As the novelty of Heyboy wore off, members of the household drifted back into their normal routines. For Ninda, this meant scheming for ways to right the world's wrongs and playing her bagpipes. At present she was doing these things simultaneously.

Dressed in her customary uniform of a camouflage jacket with the collar torn out and a flat red cap, she stood before her bedroom window practicing for the upcoming kumquat growers' rally. Ninda plays the bagpipes as an instrument of protest because she believes that in order to get any attention, protest must be loud.

Most of the Bellweather household doesn't seem to mind the music. Predictably, the one member of the family who does mind is the one prone to towering rages (or outbursts of an outlandish sense of humor) and busy eyebrows, Dr. Bellweather. He is a man who seems oblivious, insensible really, to the chaos around him when he is not working, but as soon as he goes into his lab and shuts the door behind him, he says that it is as if every sound in the household is magnified beyond the roar of a jet engine. He claims to have soundproofed his lab, but the blare of the foghorn and the screech of the bagpipes continue to seep through.

In her sixth-floor bedroom, Ninda enjoys practicing "Let my People Go." In his fifth-floor laboratory, her father is warmed by irritation. She works on "Amazing Grace." Her father simmers with aggravation. She plays "If I Had a Hammer." Her father boils with rage.

Finally, matters came to a head. Dr. Bellweather was grumpier than usual at having missed hitting a visitor with a set of glass beakers and evidently decided that *someone* would have to pay for disturbing his concentration. He burst into Ninda's bedroom with such force that her framed picture of the famous labor leader, Nate King—who organized a union for coal miners who would only work above ground— was knocked off the wall.

The photo had been given to Ninda by Grandma Paisley. It was she who had first encouraged Ninda to develop a social conscience. Several years ago, Spider had been coming into his own as a computer genius (Eel-Smack-by-the-Bay's local newspaper had done a feature article on him after he set up a system for the local library), and the triplets were cute (and destructive) in a way that seemed to capture everyone's interest. Grandma Paisley sensed a case of middle-child-itis coming over her granddaughter and casually mentioned that Ninda could distinguish herself by Doing Good and Being Kind.

Of course, Ninda has been accused of taking things rather further than the average person might.*

At first she didn't notice her father's intrusion; her back was to the door. Dr. Bellweather had to get

---

*She once shaved her head to demonstrate sympathy for the shampoo girls at the village beauty salon. Ninda marched around in front of the Glamour-a-Go-Go for two weeks, until the exasperated owner finally raised the wages of the girls who worked for him. He claimed afterward that it was just coincidence, that the pay raise had been planned all along, but Ninda never believed him.

right in front of her and jump up and down to get her attention.

Ninda looked up at him, her mouth on the blow-pipe, which is the part of the bagpipe that one blows into to produce the screechy sound. The part of the instrument which wheezes and sounds like a cow with asthma is called the hide bag.

Perhaps Ninda should have taken a hint from her instrument and hidden.

"I said stop that racket!" Dr. Bellweather shouted.

"Yelling is unkind," Ninda said, removing the blowpipe from her mouth.

"I'm not yelling!" shouted her father. "And if I were, you couldn't have heard me anyway! No one can hear a blasted thing in this house with that infernal noise!"

"You never say anything when the triplets make noise!" Ninda accused.

"A brilliant scientist such as myself becomes accustomed to working against a backdrop of mechanical noises!"

Dr. Bellweather's face was red; his busy eyebrows began to quiver. "Hammering and explosions fade into nothing. Bagpipe music does not!" The busy eyebrows stretched.

"Do you enjoy having a roof over your head and food to eat? Because here's the situation: if I can't concentrate, I can't work; if I can't work, I don't receive money; if I don't receive money, I can't pay the bills; and if I can't pay the bills, we will be tossed, destitute and famished, into the street."

"What are you working on now?" she asked, laying aside her instrument. Redirection usually worked well on Dr. Bellweather.

"I'm *trying* to design a device to wash the windows in high-rise buildings." His eyebrows quieted down. "Balfour Justice asked me to see what I could do about that." Dr. Bellweather pointed out the window to a tall building nestled in the heart of Eel-Smack-by-the-Bay, which was sprawled out at the foot of the hill.

Ninda knew Mr. Justice well. He himself had an active social conscience. He was an attorney who took a great interest in workers' rights, often taking on their cases for free. Of course, he could afford to be generous; he was also the proud owner of the tallest building in Eel-Smack-by-the-Bay.

Although the structure was a bit of a distance away from them, Ninda could see huge splotches of color on it.

"Some idiot filled water balloons with paint, and then fired them at the top of the building. He must have used a high-pressure device. What a mess." Dr. Bellweather shook his head. Ninda shook her head, too. She'd warned the triplets about using their motor-driven, super-velocity slingshots.

"Avery Snubb makes his living washing windows. It would be unkind to take work away from him," Ninda pronounced, her clear blue eyes narrowing and darkening.

"Last month his scaffolding broke with him on it—now he only washes the windows he can reach by leaning out of the building," Dr. Bellweather told her. "He says he'll sue Justice if he gets fired. Claims his new fear of heights is a disability. Wouldn't that be something—Balfour (Human Rights) Justice, sued by a laborer?" Dr. Bellweather chuckled.

"I'm sure you'll think of something for the windows," Ninda said, interrupting her father's amusement at the expense of his old friend.

"I could if I were able to get a moment's peace in this house!" Dr. Bellweather suddenly remembered why he was in Ninda's room. His eyebrows started their warm-up. "If I hear another note out of that blasted thing, it goes out the window!"

"But I need to practice," she said.

"Not in this house," Dr. Bellweather insisted. "Do you want to reduce your poor family to having to beg on the streets?" Dr. Bellweather's eyebrows did jumping jacks. "I can see it now: We'll dress the triplets as little monkeys, and you can play your pipes for them to dance to. Spider can pass the hat, and we'll all sleep on the beach. We'll keep Benway on so he can smooth the sand in the driftwood hovel where we'll shiver away the cold winter nights." Dr. Bellweather's voice dropped low. "If things get really bad, we'll use him for food."

"But what about the kumquat workers?" Ninda asked. It's not as though she had no concern at the prospect of cannibalizing Benway. It's just that the devastating starvation of the family was a familiar theme of Dr. Bellweather's, and no one really paid much attention when he warmed to that particular subject.

"I'm not concerned with what happens to the kumquat workers. I'm concerned with what happens to *this* worker." Dr. Bellweather pointed to himself, eyebrows in a frenzied tap dance. "*This* worker needs quiet for his work, and rather than crusade for the rights of *this* worker, his ungrateful offspring prefers to torture *this* worker with an unholy noise!"

"Those people in the fields aren't the only oppressed ones around here," Ninda grumbled.

"You're right!" Dr. Bellweather came back at her. "Poor genius fathers who have too many children to feed and aren't respected in their own homes are surely as oppressed as your teeming masses! That thing"— he pointed with a shaking finger at the bagpipes—"is not to be played in this house again. No more noise!"

Just before he turned to leave the room, Ninda could have sworn she saw his eyebrows take a bow.

July 25,
GLOAT minus 5 weeks, 3 days, 3 hours, and 22 minutes

Dear Journal,

There was quite a lively discussion between Eugene Bellweather and Ninda today. I did not need to use my spy camera in order to discover the nature of the discussion. It is not my place to offer an opinion, but if it were, I'd say that Dr. Bellweather's voice, when raised in "jest," can be quite as loud as Ninda's bagpipes. She, however, shall have to practice down on the beach while her father is free to speak as loudly as he likes anywhere he pleases. (Use me for food, indeed! And I ask you, where is Ninda's famous concern for human rights when it comes to me? I didn't hear one Word of Protest escape her lips when it came to defending my poor body from her father's "outlandish sense of humor!")

Oh, yes. Ninda has vowed to take action regarding being forced to play her pipes out-of-doors. I cannot claim to know what form that action shall take, nor when it shall occur. I only know that any action ever taken by any Bellweather family member has always, and will always, result in crisis.

These musings would ordinarily fill me with a foreboding of the darkest kind. Not that this foreboding would be obvious—I pride myself on being as unflappable as the stiff, white hand-kerchief I keep bent into a triangle in my suit coat pocket. (Extra starch does the trick.) My mind, however, has turned to higher things.

My book project is coming along quite well. I have been gratified by the positive response from my friend, the editor. He has plans to bring out my book right away, by the end of the summer at the latest. This coincides nicely with the end of the Wretched Oath of Fealty, a mere 5 weeks, 3 days, 3 hours, and 18 minutes from now.

I am looking forward to the appearance of the real-estate catalog advertising Charming Cottages, Located in Warm Climates Far, Far Away. I sent for it over a week ago—surely it is due to arrive soon!

·5·
THE TRIPLETS
ENGAGE IN ART

Anyone who is familiar with twins or triplets knows that while there might be strong similarities in appearance, one can usually tell the individuals apart by some small difference. For instance, Brick Bellweather has short, curly blond hair; deceptively innocent, large blue eyes; and a dimple in his cheek. Sassy Bellweather has deceptively innocent, large blue eyes; short, curly blonde hair; and a dimple in her cheek. Spike Bellweather has a dimple in his cheek; deceptively innocent, large blue eyes; and short, curly blond hair.

Before hanging up his trench coat, he pulled a small package and a piece of mail out of the pocket. The mail was not addressed to him, nor was the package which contained plumeria seeds and instructions for growing them. Spider knew that even the Eel-Smack summers were too cool for growing these tropical flowers. The mail was a real-estate catalog advertising the sale of Charming Cottages in Warm Climates Far, Far Away. Both the catalog and the seed packet were addressed to Tristan Benway.

Now, it was possible that these items had been a mistake somehow, and Spider was not one to jump to conclusions. It did, however, seem a peculiar coincidence that *both* pieces of misaddressed mail should arrive in the same post. Could Benway be planning to leave? If so, why? Spider hid the catalog and the seed packet behind one of his computers and climbed into the hammock for a Deep Thought session, which lasted until dinnertime.

After dinner, the family scattered to their own pursuits. Lillian went back to her painting, and Ninda (with a fierce scowl at her father, which was noticed by everyone but the intended recipient) went down to the beach to play her bagpipes. Spider went back to his lair and Dr. Bellweather tried to read the evening newspaper in the red sitting room—so called, although the walls were painted chartreuse.

The professor was not having an easy time of it. The triplets, garbed in matching yellow goggles and heavy work gloves, were making modifications to the sofa upon which he reclined.

"IT SEEMS A PITY NO ONE WILL EVER SEE IT," yelled Brick, using a hacksaw on one of the legs. He was referring of course to the painting, which their own brother had taken no notice of.

"THE WORLD IS A SADDER PLACE BECAUSE OF THAT," agreed Sassy. She was cutting a zigzag pattern into one of the cushions with an X-Acto knife.

"IT FEELS ALMOST CRIMINAL," screamed Spike, who really ought to know.

Nothing more might have ever come of that conversation had Spike not started up the chainsaw.

This caused Dr. Bellweather to abandon his newspaper with an oath and stomp from the room, roaring about orphanages that would be pleased to take in triplets. Dr. Bellweather was not a coward; however, he made it policy to remove himself from the triplets' company whenever they were in possession of dangerous equipment . . . which was quite often.

Spike finished sawing off a piece of the armrest, and the triplets prepared to abandon their project—leaving the mess for someone else to clean up—when Sassy's eye fell on the front page of the newspaper.

"Look," she whispered. The hair on the necks of every living thing within a five-mile radius stood up. The headline of the newspaper read, *The Lady to Smile on Eel-Smack-by-the-Bay.*

The Global Art Exchange is a nonprofit program whose goal is to expose fine art to the common man. Several internationally famous museums have agreed to lend high-profile pieces to this traveling exhibit. The highlight of this very impressive show will be Da Vinci's masterpiece, the *Mona Lisa*, which Jean Bleujeanes, curator of the Louvre, has graciously loaned to the tour. The collection will be making a stop in Eel-Smack-by-the-Bay late this summer. Visitors are expected to throng to the Eel-Smack museum to view this and other fine paintings.

"Are you thinking what I'm thinking?" whispered Sassy to her brothers.

"If you're thinking that our masterpiece belongs on that world tour, then I am," Brick whispered back.

"If you're thinking that not many people will *really* want to see the *Mona Lisa*, then I'm thinking what you both are thinking," whispered Spike.

"If you're thinking that we should hide the *Mona Lisa*, so that the people in town don't have to look at anything but our masterpiece, we're thinking the same thing," whispered Sassy.

"If you're thinking that we should borrow it anonymously and then hide it somewhere in the museum, then I'm thinking what you are thinking," said Brick.

"After all, we'll give it back as soon as people have had a chance to notice OUR masterpiece."

"If I'm thinking the Louvre obviously doesn't mind loaning out their paintings, so it shouldn't be a problem for us to borrow it and then hide it, then I am thinking what I am thinking, too," Sassy told them.

And so it was that the triplets planned to play hide the button with one of the most famous pieces of art in the history of the world.

———————

July 28,
GLOAT minus 5 weeks, 2 hours, and 45 minutes

Dear Journal,

Although I consider it my duty to see to it that the children have the food they like to eat available to them, I do not understand the triplets' taste for chocolate syrup and carrots. Nor do I understand their appetite for destruction. The three wrecked another sofa today, but neither that nor the dreaded whispers that followed are worthy of notice. Today was a glorious day—one which brought me closer yet to the event of my escape. Today I placed the advertisement for my replacement on the Eel-Smack-by-the-Bay Community Bulletin Board.

When I arrived in town, Balfour Justice was, himself, tacking up an advertisement. After we greeted each other, he told me that he was advertising for the position of Window Washer for his building, the tallest in town.

I was reminded of Ninda's concern. "What of Avery Snubb?" I asked.

"I'll keep him on to wash the windows on the ground floor, of course." Mr. Justice looked offended at the thought that he would fire anyone—even someone who refused to do the job he'd been hired to do.

"I contracted with your employer to come up with a device to wash windows that can't be reached from the ground," he continued, as though he owed me an explanation. "I'm advertising for replacement window washers, in case Eugene's tantrums keep him from coming up with a solution to my problem." The attorney smiled rather conspiratorially at me. Most improper.

"I am sure I do not know to what you are referring," I told him, my bow as icy as was proper. Mr. Justice looked a little confused as he took my leave.

Regardless of their reputation, I do not engage in gossip against the Bellweathers. It may be Wretched, but an Oath of Fealty is an Oath of Fealty, after all. We shall see what my feelings on the subject are 5 weeks, 2 hours, and 34 minutes from now when my Glorious Oath to forever leave this family replaces the Wretched Oath to Serve.

When the attorney was safely down the street, I tacked up my little advert.

Employment Opportunity.
Wanted: One gentleman possessed of nerves of steel
and impeccable organizational skills. Applicant

must know how to set a formal dining table as
well as the best method of large-animal sedation.
Lunatic-asylum experience is helpful.
Interested parties please reply to Tristan Benway
c/o Lighthouse on the Hill.

It took Some Time to compose the message. Reading it over, I recognize that it is doubtful that anyone who graduated first in his class at an Academy for Butlers (as I may have mentioned was the case for me, personally) will answer the call.

Such concerns, though, will soon be in the past, and so my thoughts were happy ones this evening, as I swept up the remains of the sofa cushions and put away the chainsaw.

· 6 ·
A PROJECT FOR NINDA

Ninda stomped out of the Lighthouse on the Hill to practice her instrument on the beach. She was feeling spiritless and cranky. Spider had Heyboy, and the triplets were whispering happily over some art plan they had. When she wasn't trying to smooth down the hairs on the back of her neck, she was casting about for opportunities for Doing Good and Being Kind. She kept coming up empty-handed, though. People to Help seemed few and far between just now.

The sun was setting and it was getting a little chilly. This did help her mood a bit. Ninda enjoyed suffering for a cause—in this case, bagpipe practice for a rally to allow people to raise their voices in the Eel-Smack-by-the-Bay Public Library if they were in distress. She'd once yelped at the pain of a paper cut. The librarian was very sympathetic, but the other patrons were not. A bagpipe protest would Show Them!

Just as she sent the last strains of "I Turned the Volume Up, 'Cause Dewey Decimal's Got Me Down" fading into the orange-tinged sunset, Ninda caught sight of a small boat beyond the line of breaking surf. This was not remarkable in and of itself. What *was* remarkable was the fact that the little skiff was being towed behind a man who appeared to be walking on water.

It soon became evident that the man was not all-powerful because the boat was caught by a wave. The vessel was violently swamped and tumbled, and its contents crashed into the foamy water. Among canvas bags and rope-tied bundles, Ninda realized that there were at least three people caught up in the waves. She dropped her bagpipes and splashed out to help. Just as she reached the boat, a wave crashed over her and a wooden stilt cracked against her shoulder. The man hadn't been walking on water at all—he'd been using stilts!

When the wave passed, Ninda stuck her head out of the water to shake salt and sand out of her nose. She thrashed toward a particularly small set of limbs. Despite the pain in her upper arm, she grabbed them (and the torso and head to which they were connected) and made her way out of the water. A little boy shook water out of his ears and grinned at Ninda. Not at all perturbed by his misadventure, he sprang up over her head and backflipped into the arms of a petite woman who was just coming up onto the beach. She hugged the boy tightly and kissed his curly black head over and over.

Ninda peered out to see if the other two were okay. The man who had been on stilts and a boy were trying to right the skiff and hold it steady enough to throw a couple of rescued objects into it. Finally they pointed the boat at the shore and sliced it through the waves and up onto the beach. The boy stayed in the water a little longer, ducking under the surf, as though looking for something. He stuck his head above water and gave a shout before coming in to where the rest of the family were gathered around the small boat, gazing at the few possessions they had left.

The little boy said something and then pointed at Ninda. His mother rushed to Ninda and clasped her in a dramatic, if soggy, embrace. The others surged forward, speaking in a language Ninda did not understand, and patting Ninda on the head and embracing her.

"We are to thanking you," the father finally said, in heavily accented English. "Pim is strong boy, but water are strong, too—is good you get him out."

"You're welcome," Ninda said, wondering at the family's appearance.

They were dressed in clothing wholly inappropriate for a boating jaunt. The father wore a crimson shirt, which when dry must have been of a billowy fabric but was just now plastered to his body. The material criss-crossed his chest and was held in place by a wide green sash. He wore tight black pants and nothing on his feet. The mother was tiny, not much bigger than Ninda, and wore a bodysuit underneath what looked like a ballerina's tutu. Her ensemble was choked with sequins. The boys were dressed in a fashion similar to their father's, but both wore thin black slippers on their feet. In short they looked like escapees from a circus. Which they were.

"I am Viktor Balboa," the father introduced himself. "This my wife Anya is"—the woman posed artistically—"and my sons Igor"—indicating the boy about Ninda's age—"and Pim."

Igor put his fingers to his mouth and gave an eyeball-popping whistle. A loping blob came up from the water, barking like a dog. When it got closer, Ninda could see a very fancy, ruffled collar drooping around its neck. The loping blob was a trained seal.

"Elza," Igor said, as though introducing a rare jewel. Pim hugged the seal and buried his face in her fur. This, to Ninda, was a feat more remarkable than his earlier backflips; Elza stunk to high heaven. Ninda had to step back. Pim, beginning to shiver, gave the seal another hug and smiled at Ninda.

"Are you all okay?" Ninda asked.

"No!" Anya was emphatic. "Cold it is, and we are tired."

"Shall we build a fire?" she asked.

"We are not liking to trouble you . . . ," Viktor said, then trailed off as Mrs. Balboa gave a violent shake—and maybe a bit of a dirty look—toward her husband.

Ninda, Viktor, and Igor collected driftwood and soon had a small bonfire going. Mrs. Balboa stood to the side, clutching Pim and Elza and shivering in a most dramatic way.

Soon everyone was drying out, and Viktor Balboa told his family's tale.

"We come from Rhinnestaadt," he said. "Is very poor country. Unstable. Always there are revolution-ings, demonstratings against the government."

Ninda smiled. Rhinnestaadt sounded like her kind of place.

"We take job with circus to come here. For one year worked for Marvolo and Brothers," Viktor said.

"I've heard of them," she said. She'd seen the circus advertised a few weeks previously.

"Ivan Marvolo is bad man!" Viktor exclaimed.

"Ee is TERRRRIBLE!" Mrs. Balboa drew out the word in fine dramatic style. "In eight months what does he pay? Nothing almost!"

"True, he pays only little," Mr. Balboa said. "Also, he keeps our passports and paperworks. Without these, we cannot live and work in this country," said Mr. Balboa.

"So you've been oppressed! That's wonderful!" Ninda was excited.

Viktor Balboa gave her an odd look before continuing. "This day, after the show, our passports and paperworks we take back from Marvolo. We travel now to Shelbywood. A different circus there is."

"Isn't there a union for circus workers?" Ninda asked.

The Balboas stared.

"You know, an organization that protects your rights? Makes sure your wages are guaranteed? Keeps you from having to work too many hours?"

"I think, no. No union," Balboa said.

Mrs. Balboa sighed. Wearily, dramatically. Her

husband patted her hand. "She tired of performing is," he told Ninda, "but work we must do, or go back to Rhinnestaadt. How far are we to Shelbywood?" Viktor Balboa asked.

Ninda thought hard. Shelbywood was only a few miles up the coast and it would be an easy thing for the family to get there from Eel-Smack. But mightn't the other circus exploit the poor Balboas? These people were willing to trade the oppression of one circus for what she was sure would be the terrible conditions of another. They were far from being educated about their rights as human beings. Imagine not even knowing what a union was! The Balboas *needed* Ninda to open their eyes to the vast possibilities of freedom.

Even if this required them to spend some time in captivity.

"I'm afraid it's terribly far," Ninda said. "You'll never make it there tonight." She waited for the Balboa family's faces to fall before going on.

"I think I have an idea," Ninda said as though such a notion were new to her. "You could stay with me.

I'll get you something to eat, you'll have a warm place to sleep, and we'll find a way for you to rise against your oppressors!"

"I am not knowing this thing, oppressors," said Mr. Balboa. "But are grateful for place to sleep. We go to Shelbywood in tomorrow. Is permitted by the parents of you?"

"It won't bother them a bit," Ninda assured him, thinking that what Dr. Bellweather didn't know couldn't possibly bother him, *and* that it would take much longer than a day to educate this family and encourage them to organize a union. Perhaps they should have to take some sort of exam regarding unionization and human rights before they could leave. . . .

She was brought back to earth by the snuffling noises Elza the stinky seal began to make. "Still, we'll have to be quiet." She touched her finger to her lips in a universal shushing gesture. The Balboas agreed, smiling. They didn't know that Dr. Bellweather threatened to unleash his sense of humor on anyone Ninda ever again brought to stay in the Lighthouse on the Hill. He had been quite put out by the Dusty Miller incident.

"I tell Elza stay on beach near boat. We get soon to come back," Viktor Balboa said.

"She can come, too," Ninda said. "But you must keep her very quiet."

And so it was that Ninda Bellweather came to host a troupe of Rhinnestaadtian circus performers and their trained seal in her bedroom. Weeks later she realized that an individual with a less refined understanding of the situation might substitute the words "hold prisoner" for "host."

———⋙•⋘———

July 29,
GLOAT minus 4 weeks, 6 days, 1 hour, and 20 minutes

Dear Journal,

Someone tracked sand all over the entryway to the lighthouse this evening. I'm not complaining. It is, after all, a common enough occurrence and a small thing compared to what I have endured over the years. Did I complain every time I found that hobos had taken over my bed? No, I did not. Did I whine when the professor hurled a Bunsen burner at my head simply because I tried to deliver a parcel to him at an inopportune time? How was I to know he HAD been on the verge of a breakthrough (he says) in the theory of perpetual motion??? No, I did not!!!!

I have endured these things and worse. Endured them without complaint of any kind. An Oath of Fealty is an Oath of Fealty. I am not one who takes the notion of loyalty lightly . . . and in any case, I have always been too hard at work to find the time to complain. . . . My only solace in certain memories of this insane asylum is that they have made for interesting chapters in my tell-all book.

I am Quite Out of Sorts, and I realize that this is partly due to my growing concern regarding the securing of my replacement. What sane man, not under the burden of a Wretched Oath of Fealty, would agree to employment with such a family? The situation is impossible.

One of the largest difficulties my would-be successor will face is due to Dr. Bellweather himself. He is very fair in choosing targets for his blustering, ranting, and glass-beaker throwing. Anyone is fair game. The villagers in Eel-Smack-by-the-Bay do not share his "sense of humor." In addition to seeing to the creature comforts of this family, the duties of my replacement will include occasionally convincing townsfolk not to riot on the Bellweathers' property. This is a task that anyone not subjected to a Wretched Oath of Fealty will unlikely be willing to perform. In fact, anyone not bound by such an oath may end up joining those rioting.

Nonetheless, before my escape—4 weeks, 6 days, 1 hour, and 17 minutes from now— I must do my utmost to find an individual possessed of the steel nerve necessary to deal with this family. I've yet to receive any response from the advertisement for my replacement which I put up on the Community Bulletin Board, but surely there is Some Individual in the area who has not heard tales of this family.

On second thought, I believe it may be prudent to advertise abroad.

I shall not, however, forgo my duties to this family while I am still in their employ. I must remember to check on Ninda before turning in, as I fear she's caught a nasty cold. There's been a terrible, barking cough coming from her room this evening.

· 7 ·

EDUCATING THE BALBOAS

Several days into the Balboas' "visit," Ninda woke early. It felt like forever since she'd enjoyed a good night's sleep. The stench of the seal and the snores of Pim were disturbing to her slumber.

Anya and Viktor Balboa were stretched out on Ninda's huge four-poster bed. Igor, covered by a blanket that had been liberated from Benway's room, slept on the floor next to the bed. His back was to Pim, who snoozed with his mouth open, tonsils vibrating, and one arm thrown carelessly over the side of Elza the seal.

Ninda creaked across the floor and out into the hall, grateful that the family was still asleep. That Anya Balboa was a complainer, and none of the family seemed too interested in the pamphlets that Ninda read to them from ten to noon and four to six. This was too bad, since a lot of that material would be appearing on the test Ninda had decided they would have to pass before they could leave. The exam would be created by Ninda herself and ensure that the Balboas knew how to do things properly and in a democratic fashion.

Today she planned to pick up a copy of the book that had helped shape her outlook, *I Am Worker, Hear Me Roar*, at the library. Once the family had read it, they would surely come around.

She made her way down to the kitchen, stepping over the remains of the triplets' latest artistic endeavor. (How *would* Benway get the tar off the chandelier once it had cooled?) From somewhere up above she heard someone trying to start a chainsaw and realized that the piece of art she was stepping over was not yet complete.

Benway was in the kitchen, surrounded by quite a few broken dishes. He wasn't sweeping the floor so much as stabbing at it with the broom. He didn't turn around when she entered, but he must have heard her.

"It seems to me that if more provisions than what are accounted for in the household budget are needed, then a Certain Individual ought to notify the person responsible for going to market," Benway said, over the savage clink of china.

"Boy, having an Endangered Albino Alligator around the house makes food disappear pretty fast," Ninda tried.

"That food is now taken into account in the budget." Benway was severe. "Food that goes missing beyond that has not. When Dr. Bellweather comes down for an anchovy-and-cracker snack and can only find maple syrup and hard-boiled eggs, he unleashes his sense of humor on the individual he considers responsible for the larder. Courtesy would indicate that a Certain Individual might alert Someone Else about the missing food ahead of time, in order to spare Someone Else the ordeal of dodging plates and cups."

"Those triplets sure . . . ," Ninda attempted again. Benway turned to face her.

"In the past several days, this household has mysteriously lost not one, not two, but *three* legs of lamb. We have gone through five heads of lettuce, seven loaves of bread, five pounds of apples, three dozen chocolate chip cookies, and no fewer than twenty-six cans of tuna fish." He smiled, faintly. "It's almost as though someone is feeding an entire family and their performing sea mammal."

Ninda could only stare. How *did* Benway always know these things?

"But you haven't . . . ?" Ninda jerked her head up in the general direction of Dr. Bellweather's office.

"Mentioned something that isn't any of my business to a certain other member of the household?" Benway finished her question, then added, "No, I have not. And I will not. It is my business to be discreet." He turned his back on Ninda and continued to sweep.

A grateful Ninda had the brief thought that not

every butler in the world would take Benway's position on discretion, particularly when it came to the activities of the younger members of the household. She shook her head—maybe it had something to do with his having graduated first in his class.

Five minutes later, after apologizing profusely to Benway, Ninda returned to her bedroom. She'd have offered to help sweep up the mess, but there wasn't time. She had overworked people to help.

The family was awake. Anya Balboa reclined on the bed. Igor sat bolt upright on the window seat. Pim was in a headstand next to the bureau and Ninda could see Elza the trained seal just through the open door of Ninda's bathroom. All of Elza's time in the bathtub certainly wasn't improving anything odor-wise.

Viktor Balboa was pacing the curved length of the room but halted when Ninda set down half a watermelon, a loaf of bread (no time to toast it), and five cans of tuna for Elza. Five pairs of eyes (four pairs human, one pair pinniped) were trained on Ninda.

Clearly, an *important discussion* had taken place in her absence.

She walked over to the bed and handed Anya Balboa a half-eaten box of chocolates. "Here's breakfast."

Noticing that she herself was the only person in the room with a smile on her face, Ninda began to chatter.

"I figure the plan for today is that you'll stay here, being very quiet and reading these pamphlets. We can talk about any questions you have," she said. "We'll all nap this afternoon, and then tonight when it gets dark, we can take turns going out on to the beach so you can practice your routines."

Ninda had warned the performers that they needed to remain hidden during daylight hours because there were people called "Immigration Officials" who would send the family back to Rhinnestaadt. Viktor pointed out that his family had all of their paperwork in order, so this shouldn't be a problem. Ninda (very smoothly, she thought) told him of the Corrupt Immigration Officials, who would steal the family's paperwork then demand bribes in order to let them stay. "It's terrible, but it happens all the time," she said. Viktor and Anya were concerned. If they had to give up their money, how were they to live while they looked for another circus?

Squaring his shoulders, Viktor decided that his family would just have to take their chances. "We are to thanking you for all you have done. Very grateful, but rest we have had for many, many days," he said. "It is time we go now."

"Of course. Of course," Ninda agreed. "But you need MORE rest for the trip. It's so far away." A similar conversation had taken place the day before. When that discussion was over, Ninda had read to the family from a text titled "Your Boss Is from Pluto: How Unionizing Will Bring Him Back to Earth."

She turned her back on Viktor and began slicing the watermelon. The very fact that the Balboas were still anxious to join the circus in Shelbywood told Ninda that they were not free of their oppressed mindset.

"In fact," she said, handing a slice of watermelon to

Pim and one to Igor, "I just found out that the circus has moved on from Shelbywood."

She plopped the five open cans of tuna on the floor in front of Elza, who snuffled at them and then scarfed down the contents.

"I need time to find out where it's gone, so I can help you get there. Also there's the matter of the unionization test. I'm sure that with a *leetle* more study, you'll all pass brilliantly!" Ninda smiled at Anya Balboa in what she hoped was an innocent and reassuring way. Mrs. Balboa popped a chocolate in her mouth, never taking her eyes off the girl.

Viktor ignored the issue of the test for the moment.

"We will find the circus," he said.

"I'm sure you could," Ninda said, "but it will take you a lot longer. And then there's always the danger of those Corrupt Immigration Officials." Ninda screwed her face into a concerned expression.

She picked up the bread and handed it to him, then headed out the door.

"I'll go right now. It really is best that you allow me to do this for you." She quickly closed the door behind her. "It's no trouble at all," she called from the hallway.

Ninda stood at the bottom of the staircase and watched for a few moments. She could hear the buzz of the chainsaw from up above. Sure enough, a moment later, when Viktor Balboa cautiously stuck his head out the door, the triplets came charging down the stairs—shrieking above the roar of the chainsaw. They were intent on finishing their latest project, but Mr. Balboa obviously thought they were intent on finishing *him*. He pulled his head inside Ninda's room quickly.

Ninda smiled. With the chainsaw buzzing in the hallway, she knew the family would be content to remain her guests a little longer.

———⟫●⟪———

August 2,
GLOAT minus 4 weeks, 2 days, 4 hours, and 13 minutes

Dear Journal,

This week has been one of the more trying ones in my career with the Bellweathers.

Quite a lot of food went missing. Dr. Bellweather blamed me, of course, causing me to reflect on Benway Family Honor. We have always kept our word—though I cannot help but consider the idea that my ancestors must have had an easier time of it than I.

After reviewing video footage (I must emphasize again that I use this method only in order to serve the family) I was able to discover what was happening to the family's provisions.

I took it in stride. I do not understand Ninda. Nor, for that matter, do I understand any of the Bellweathers . . . but nothing they do can surprise me. I daresay that won't be the case with the chap who replaces me. Not that there have been any applicants so far. Perhaps I ought to rethink the wording of the advertisement I put up.

Dealing with this family takes wisdom and maturity; one must keep a calm head. No Easy

Thing for some whippersnapper. He's out there somewhere. . . . I imagine he's young, fresh-faced, and optimistic. We'll just have to see how those qualities hold up under the ravages of servitude to this family.

Come to think of it, happily enough, in 4 weeks, 2 days, 4 hours, and 11 minutes, I won't be around to see. I'm certain that compared to Dr. Bell-weather's sure-to-be-outrageous reaction when he discovers the contents of my book, broken crockery will seem tame in comparison!

THE TRIPLETS ASK FOR HELP

Spike, Sassy, and Brick puzzled (in a gleeful way, of course) the best method for pulling off what they had come to refer to as their "Private Art Exchange." It was their favorite topic of discussion while they were out on their rounds of destruction and mayhem.

"There will be some difficulty in bringing our masterpiece into the museum without notice," Sassy whispered to Brick and Spike as they poured cement into an automobile in order to make a cast of the backseat.

And later:

"I believe the difficulty will be in the actual removal of the *Mona Lisa*," Brick whispered to the other two as they smashed the windows in the gardener's shed with rag-tied rocks. They needed shards of glass for yet another mixed-media piece they were planning.

Later yet:

"I should think we would have to wait until nighttime, when no one is around, so that we won't be noticed borrowing the one and replacing it with the other," whispered Spike to Sassy and Brick as they crouched in some shrubbery and watched the telephone man replace some wires that had been mysteriously snipped.

"We are going to need help," Sassy concluded as they trudged up Lighthouse Hill. The late-afternoon sun was settling back into the horizon across the water. The day had been a frenzied one, even by the triplets' standards, and they were a little tired.

"Shall we ask Ninda?" whispered Brick. There was no danger of his being overheard; he was just Up to No Good.

"She'll just ask how much the night watchman

gets paid and then make us help her protest until his wages are increased," whispered Spike.

And so they left the warm, fading sunlight for the cool dank of Spider's lair.

After stopping by the bathroom to rub Heyboy behind the ears, they found Spider stretched out in his hammock. Thinking (and frowning) Deeply.

When Spider finally opened his eyes, Spike whispered, "We need your help."

"Doing what?" Spider asked. He gave the wall a little push with his foot, which caused the hammock to swing.

"We need to get into the museum," Sassy whispered.

"You've been there plenty of times," Spider said.

"Well, we need to get in after hours," Brick told him.

"Oh, you mean you need my help to *break* into the museum," Spider said. The triplets nodded their curly blond heads. "Why?" he asked.

"We need to add our masterpiece to an exhibit," Sassy whispered.

"Anonymously," Spike added, leaving out CER-TAIN INFORMATION.

Spider caught the slight hesitation in his sibling's voice.

"You're *just* going to add your piece?" Spider asked.

The triplets did their best to look innocent. It wasn't usually very hard to do so, but Spider was immune to this technique.

"We promise not to harm any of the pieces inside the museum," Sassy finally said. Spike and Brick nodded their heads. Surely there could be no harm in just hiding the *Mona Lisa* for a short time. And if harm were to befall the *Mona Lisa*, surely it would happen *outside* the museum.

The problem of gaining access was an intriguing one, and Spider agreed to help them.

He turned to his computer and quickly called up the blueprints for the museum and its security system. When he found what he was looking for he smiled. "The entire system relies on a single computer," he told the triplets.

"Can you hack into it?" Sassy whispered.

Spider, Brick and Spike looked at her as though they could not believe what she'd just asked.

Sassy recognized her silliness immediately. "Sorry," she said.

"That's okay," Spider said. "I won't need to hack it at all. This is definitely a job for the three of you."

"How's that?" asked Brick.

"Do we get to detonate a bomb?" asked Spike. The triplets enjoyed the good shiver that the words *detonate* and *bomb* always induced in them.

"I think that would harm the other paintings, don't you?" Spider asked. Three sets of shoulders slumped.

"We won't," they grumbled.

"At night the exhibits in the fine-art wing are guarded by infrared beams. When the beams are interrupted, an alarm will sound. The nimrod who designed the system has all of the signals feeding into one computer," Spider told them.

"All you three need to do is get past the night watchman, disable the computer, and add your piece to the exhibit."

"First we need to case the joint," Spike whispered. He had heard that line in a gangster movie once and had been itching to utter it ever since.

And so the triplets began in earnest to plan their assault on the world of art.

——»•«——

August 4,
GLOAT minus 4 weeks, 4 hours, and 27 minutes

Dear Journal,

I am feeling uneasy, despite my loftier concerns. Those triplets are Up to No Good. I have a keenly honed sense for such things. It has been developed over years spent serving this family. Such a sense will most definitely be missing in a newcomer. Speaking of which, someone has finally responded to my advert.

I received a telephone call from a chap named Wodehouse Smithers. (An unlikely name if ever there was one.) He'd seen my notice on the Community Bulletin Board a week ago, but didn't respond right away. (I wonder if this is a sign of indecisiveness, perhaps indicating a weak character.) Nevertheless, he remembered that the posting was for a butler at the Lighthouse on the Hill. He rang here to find out if the position had been filled, and I am to meet with him on my day off.

It occurs to me that even if he is a butler of good reputation (and willing to put up with the antics of this brood), it is unlikely that he will be capable of handling matters as well as I have. Indeed, it may be unlikely that he is able to handle them at all. Still, a mere 4 weeks, 4 hours, and 25 minutes from now, the matters involved in the running of this household will be None of My Business!

·9·

SPIDER MAKES A DISCOVERY AND A MISTAKE

The day after he had helped the triplets, Spider made a discovery. It happened just after Heyboy's walk (which was always done on the beach side of the Lighthouse on the Hill to avoid the prying eyes of Thaddeus Bohack).

Upon coming back into the house, Heyboy was still in frisky mood, so they played a little fetch in the wide front hall. There are several fine portraits and family heirlooms in the front hall, and some might think it a mistake to play fetch there. Especially when the fetcher is an Endangered Albino Alligator who is, from snout to tail, the length of a Cub Scout and a half.

Among the finer objects stands a rather nasty-looking, weather-beaten grandfather clock. Members of the family had variously noticed and commented that it was the only thing in the Lighthouse on the Hill that Benway refused to polish.

Spider threw the rubber ball long, and Heyboy had to turn around to go after it. His tail smacked the clock, causing its door to spring open.

"Easy, boy," Spider admonished, going over to close the door, which he had trouble doing. He bent closer to see if perhaps the hinges had been bent, and saw a small wooden container. It had obviously slipped out of its position inside of the clock. Curious, he removed the box, closed the clock, and sought the privacy of his lair, where he could examine his find more closely. He left Heyboy to roam freely about the Lighthouse on the Hill, making messes on the furniture, snapping at people, and raiding the larder, before he, too, headed down to the lair.

Once inside his room, Spider worked to slide the

top off the wooden box. Nestled inside was a scroll. Hoping against intellect that he held in his hands a pirate map (imagine the endangered beasts he could help with all of that gold!), he unrolled the parchment very slowly, and taking care not to crumple its flaky edges, he read the Benway Family

OATH OF FEALTY

Spider was aghast. He rolled up the parchment quickly, placing it back in its box and hiding it with the seed packet and real-estate catalog advertising Charming Cottages in a Warm Climate Far, Far Away.

Was it possible that Benway knew of this pledge? He himself had never heard of it. Spider crept into his hammock and closed his eyes. The Bellweathers were not a clan given to introspection, and Spider was no exception. He had never really given much thought to *why* Benway remained in their employ. Benway was just Benway, in the way that the triplets were just the triplets, except that he was taller and less destructive than they were.

Spider considered the matter for some time, and when he finally opened his eyes, the triplets were there in front of him, waiting for him to come out of his Deep Thought session.

Spider Bellweather considers himself to be extremely intelligent. Being so bright prevents him from making many mistakes. For instance, he never sticks his hands inside of beehives, he never tries to prank-call the president of the United States of America, and he never wears his raincoat into the ocean.

Intelligence, however, is no hedge against *all* mistakes, and Spider did end up making a rather large one. When he later forced himself to admit this, it comforted him to think that he wouldn't have made it at all had he not been so distracted by the discovery of the Oath of Fealty.

The request was simple. "Would you please feed Heyboy?"

The triplets looked at one another. They were enchanted by their assignment.

"OF COURSE!" screamed Sassy.

"YOU GOT IT!" shouted Brick.

"THIS IS GOING TO BE MORE FUN THAN POKING HOLES IN PERSIAN RUGS WITH WIRE COAT HANGERS!" rejoiced Spike.

The three had been working on a still life with artichokes, in the hopes of adding another piece to their Private Art Exchange. When they brought the spiky veggies down to the bathroom of the lair, the alligator was unimpressed by their offering. He closed his eyes and took a nap. This perplexed the triplets. After all, they loved artichokes, which they ate with great quantities of peanut butter and whipped cream.

"WHY DOESN'T HE EAT?" Brick shrieked to Spider.

"HE'S OFF HIS FEED," Spike yelled.

"What'd you give him?" Spider called, not looking up from his computer.

"LOVELY, LOVELY ARTICHOKES," Sassy screamed.

"He's not a vegetarian," Spider explained.

"OH!"

"RIGHT, THEN!"

"WE'LL BE BACK!" The triplets stampeded up the stairs and out into the yard.

Within half an hour they were back downstairs with Heyboy's lunch. It is unfortunate that lunch in this case had to be led down to the lair on a leash.

Ninda meanwhile had come downstairs, too. Spider considered asking her if she thought Benway was unhappy—but before he could find the right way to do so without revealing what he had learned so far, she asked for help looking up techniques for "Encouraging Cooperation." She told him she felt that the term "Mind Control" had an ugly connotation.

The computer was always a welcome distraction to Spider. Concern for Benway's emotional health faded, and soon he and Ninda were lost in research, and completely unaware of the drama unfolding in the hallway behind them.

The German shepherd must have caught a whiff of Heyboy, because he sat down suddenly and refused to budge. The triplets tried tugging on his collar to get him to move but soon gave up. They considered themselves tenderhearted, and had no wish to hurt the dog's neck. Instead, Brick held the leash while Spike and Sassy pushed from behind. The dog's nails left deep grooves in the wooden floor. This didn't concern them in the least, and why should it have? It wasn't *their* job to polish the floor.

When they reached the door of the bathroom, the dog's quiet whimper increased in volume until it became a howl. This became piercing as the distance between the door and the bathtub where Heyboy snoozed narrowed. Spider and Ninda came running to see what the racket was.

"Suffering laborer!" Ninda cried when she saw what was happening.

"What in the name of binary code is going on here?" Spider demanded.

"WE'RE FEEDING HEYBOY," Brick and Spike yelled.

"DOG FOOD!" shouted Sassy with pride.

It is a good thing for the dog that Heyboy was

a deep sleeper. It is unlikely that even Spider could have intervened otherwise.

"Now hold on a minute," Spider said, catching sight of the cowering dog's collar. "Is this the neighbor's dog?"

Spike quickly stepped between Spider and the dog. "NO," he shouted.

"NOT AT ALL," yelled Sassy.

"WHAT MAKES YOU THINK THAT?" Brick screamed.

"His dog tags," Spider said.

The triplets nodded their heads, as though considering the matter.

"HE'S NOT," shouted Spike. "BUT SUPPOSING HE WAS, WELL THEN, WHAT'D HAPPEN?"

"I'd tell you to take him straight back down the hill again. I can't believe you three. You never think beyond what you're doing, or of anyone else's feelings!" Spider had a momentary twinge of discomfort. Not only was he unused to scolding the triplets, but it came home to him that until this very day he had never considered that Benway had any feelings at all.

Spider grew warm under the stares of his siblings. He wasn't ready to share his discovery with them until he had figured out what it meant for himself. This had less to do with prudence for the sake of prudence than it did with an extreme dislike of being proved wrong about anything.

"I mean, what if someone tried to take Heyboy and feed him to their pet?" he asked.

"IT WOULDN'T WORK 'CAUSE HEYBOY'D EAT THEIR PET FIRST!" Sassy screamed.

"IF HE HADN'T ALREADY EATEN THE PERSON WHO STOLE HIM!" Brick yelled.

Ninda nodded. "They have a point," she said.

Spider shook his head. "You three had better take him home now," he said. "Find something else to feed Heyboy. And no livestock," he added.

The triplets rolled their deceptively innocent blue eyes at him. "YOU SHOULD HAVE TOLD US THAT IN THE FIRST PLACE!" they yelled.

August 6,

GLOAT minus 3 weeks, 5 days, 4 hours, and 22 minutes

Dear Journal,

My back aches from polishing the wooden floor in the lair. It has somehow become grooved. When I inquired of Spider how this came to be, I was Quite Surprised by his reaction. He mumbled something about dog food and I observed an expression upon his face that I have <u>never</u> seen on the face of anyone in the Bellweather clan. It was an unmistakable Look of Guilt.

Unusual, considering the complete sense of justification the Bellweathers have about <u>all</u> of their actions—never noticing when said actions have a Negative Impact on those around them. Indeed, with the exception of Ninda, they demonstrate not the faintest concern for anyone but themselves, and I believe Ninda's concern to be motivated by equal parts charity and attention grubbing.

Allegiance to an Oath of Fealty is difficult

enough to bear for a thinking man who graduated first in his class (as I believe I may have mentioned I did). The fact that the Bellweathers have never appreciated the hard work that befalls me due to their antics has necessarily made bearing the burden of the Wretched Oath of Fealty that much more difficult.

In other matters, the tell-all book project continues along quite nicely. There was (unfortunately) a wealth of material. However, the fine chaps at the publishing house helped me to whittle it down so as to make it a manageable size. It won't be too much longer before the secrets of the Bellweathers are revealed. And in 3 weeks, 5 days, 4 hours, and 20 minutes, I shall be free.

It is Not Amusing to think that Spider may be Developing a Conscience just in time for my replacement to enjoy it. Not that I would permit personal feeling to ever enter into a professional relationship. This family's lack of regard for <u>me</u> and my feelings is of no consequence. Truly.

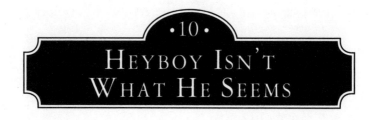

·10·
HEYBOY ISN'T
WHAT HE SEEMS

Heyboy was a good influence, Spider thought. He'd read that captive Endangered Albino Alligators need exercise every day and briefly considered asking one of his siblings to walk Heyboy, but Ninda was always either holed up in her room or spending a lot of time on mysterious errands to the library. It is only natural that after the dog-food incident, he didn't trust the triplets to do anything.

Thus Spider was forced into the great outdoors for exercise once a day. He knew that the sight of a boy in a trench coat, hat, and sunglasses, holding a leash with an Endangered Albino Alligator on the business end of it was an interesting one, probably best viewed from a distance.

Careful spying had taught him that Thaddeus Bohack was a creature of habit. Every day Bohack had lunch at Barnacle Bill's Pretty Okay Diner from one to two o'clock. This then became the time when Spider and Heyboy would stroll down the coast side of the hill and walk along the beach. Heyboy loved the daily walks; he even learned to take his leash in his mouth and bring it to Spider when it was time to go.

One day, however, Heyboy refused to get out of the bathtub for a walk.

Spider had been absorbed in his online research of the Endangered Winged Cobra.*

Captivated and enchanted, he didn't notice that

---

*Winged Cobra is a misnomer. These snakes simply have overdeveloped hoods (that's the big part that sticks out around their heads before they strike) that act as parachutes. The cobras slither up baobab trees, uncoil themselves from the branches quickly, and then puff out their hoods, soaring through the air like flying squirrels. Unlike the flying squirrel, however, the Winged Cobra uses this method of locomotion to land on its prey, sink its fangs into the neck, and kill its victim with one bite. The bite of the Endangered Winged Cobra is always fatal.

walk time had come and gone. It was the blare of the foghorn that finally roused him from his computer.

Upstairs he could hear Balfour Justice asking Dr. Bellweather if the window-washing device was ready yet. Down in the valley below, villagers in Eel-Smack-by-the-Bay could probably hear Dr. Bellweather roaring that, no, the by-jingoed invention was not ready yet, because people like Balfour were constantly distracting him. The shouting was followed by the sound of something metallic clanging to the ground.

When quiet was eventually restored, Spider realized it was well past lunchtime. He went looking for Heyboy. A quick circuit around the Lighthouse on the Hill would have to suffice for today's walk.

He found the alligator in the tub.

"C'mon, Heyboy, it's time for your walkie," Spider said, then glanced over his shoulder. He believed no one knew he talked baby talk to the animal. Spider goo-gooed at the beast for a minute and then picked up the leash.

"How come ooo didn't get ooo's iddle leash for walkies? Hmmm?"

Heyboy regarded Spider placidly but made no move to get up.

"Come on, buddy. Time for walkies."

Heyboy remained where he was.

"Is ooo a tired boy? Is hims a lazy boy?" Spider reached down and rubbed the gator's head for a minute. "Okay, boy. It's time to go," he said, sliding the leash around Heyboy's neck and giving it a gentle tug. Heyboy didn't yield. When Spider tugged again, Heyboy snapped his teeth.

"Hey!" Spider was surprised. "That's not okay," he said, flicking Heyboy's snout with his thumb and forefinger. Heyboy lowered his head, shamed. This time when Spider gave the leash a tug, Heyboy slowly rose to his feet and leaned to one side, revealing the bottom of the tub. Spider gasped. There, underneath the alligator, were four glistening, fist-sized eggs.

Just then, Ninda charged down the steps to the lair waving an advertisement. Taking no notice of the eggs, she shoved the paper into Spider's hands.

"Just look what I found!" She was breathless. "It was on the Community Bulletin Board!" The paper read:

Employment Opportunity.
Wanted: One gentleman possessed of nerves of steel
and impeccable organizational skills. Applicant
must know how to set a formal dining table as
well as the best method of large-animal sedation.
Lunatic-asylum experience is helpful.
Interested parties please reply to Tristan Benway
c/o Lighthouse on the Hill.

"What can he mean by this?" she asked.

Spider didn't answer her. He read the notice again and then looked up. "Go find the triplets," he said. The Bellweather children were not given to holding family meetings, but this situation clearly called for it.

Ten minutes later, Ninda was back downstairs, the triplets in tow. On her way to their art studio, she'd poked her head into her bedroom and made a shushing noise at the Balboas. "Corrupt Immigration Officials," she'd mouthed at the startled family before going off to find the triplets. She'd been away longer than she liked to be and had wanted to ensure that they'd still be there when she got back.

She found the unholy alliance whispering. When they all got downstairs, the hair on the back of her neck was still standing up.

The three noticed the eggs immediately.

"JOLLY GOOD," Brick shouted.

"CONGRATULATIONS, BOY," yelled Spike.

"WHY DIDN'T YOU TELL US HEYBOY WAS GOING TO BE A FATHER?" screamed Sassy.

"He's not," Spider said, leading the way out of the bathroom. "It seems that Heyboy is Heygirl. She's going to be a mother." The joy he felt at this development was overshadowed by an uncomfortable feeling that Benway was going to be even more likely to want to leave now.

The others followed Spider back into his room. With great ceremony, he retrieved from behind the computer the evidence he had amassed. The tropical seed packet and the advertisement for Charming Cottages in Warm Climates Far, Far Away. He took the Oath of Fealty out of its box and very gently unrolled it on the desk. The others crowded around.

When he was sure that all had had a chance to

finish reading, he tapped the date in the upper right-hand corner.

"Notice anything?" he asked.

"The two hundred years are nearly up!" Ninda tried to digest the notion that Benway, far from choosing to work for the family of his own free will, was really an indentured servant. "This is ridiculous! Surely a man of Benway's intelligence would see this is unenforceable!"

"Why else would he stay on?" Spider asked.

The children looked at one another. Why indeed? Visions of wild animals and cut-up clothing and vagrants at the dinner table flashed through their heads.

"WE'D STAY!" the triplets shouted.

"Yes, but we're talking about Benway. It's obvious that he's planning to leave," Spider said, and the children were silent for a moment, each trying to imagine what a life without Benway would be like.

"I always ask him if he's feeling Downtrodden or Exploited and he's never hinted that he was unhappy," Ninda finally said.

"The point is, he's planning to leave, and we've got to convince him not to." Spider was emphatic. "I've already decided that I'll find another location for an Endangered Albino Alligator Habitat. Once Heyboy—Heygirl, I mean—isn't nipping at him all the time, he might be more comfortable. . . ."

"I'm sure I don't know what more I can do for him," Ninda said. "After all, I've always been kind to him. I'll have to think about it when I'm done with my current project."

"Well, figure out something quick—September the first is coming up." Spider turned to the triplets, who'd been nudging one another and communicating with their eyebrows. "You three had better consider what you can do to help, too."

"Oh, we'll find something to make him stay," Spike whispered, leading Sassy and Brick out of the lair without elaborating on this point. It was obvious the three had already decided (in that frightening non-verbal way they had) not to include Ninda and Spider in their plan.

Spider smoothed the hair on the back of his neck,

while Ninda tried to ignore the tingling of hers.

"I can't believe he wants to leave," she said. "Besides, where would he go?"

Spider handed her the plumeria seed packet and the real-estate catalog.

"Far, far away," he told her.

———⇒⊃●⊂⇐———

August 7,
GLOAT minus 3 weeks, 4 days, 2 hours, and 22 minutes

Dear Journal,

That brute has managed to reproduce itself! Heyboy is a Heygirl. Spider, though he seems cautious not to make it too obvious, is delighted. If anyone expects me to play nursemaid to hatchling beasts of carnage . . . Heygirl indeed!

I do not understand the joy Spider feels at the prospect of five Endangered Albino Alligators running loose about the lighthouse. It is not one

I cherish. Of course it is not a servant's place to come right out and state what he or she thinks, and I hold to that position. However, I believe it is perfectly acceptable, even by one bound by a Wretched Oath, to hint at one's feelings. This takes a great deal of subtlety. Which is always lost on this family . . . I wonder how long it will take the fellow who replaces me to figure that out.

My successor will very like be Wodehouse Smithers (he of the unlikely name and possibly weak character). I met with him in town today. By remarkable coincidence, it seems that we attended the same academy. I must say, that on the surface, he would appear to be an ideal candidate, although he himself did not graduate first in his class as I did. Oh, he _is_ young and fresh-faced and optimistic. In fact he is just as I imagined him to be.

We met at "Tuxedos and Ice Cream," that venerable institution which serves as an informal gathering place for the few of us in service to families of Eel-Smack-by-the-Bay. Some may find two such goods for sale in the same establishment to be at odds—but the union was born when Eel-Smack's only tailor, Jeremiah Stitch, married the Widow Goodmallow, owner of the village sweetshop. There are those who find it nice to have a little "pick-me-up" treat after the serious business of properly outfitting oneself has been attended to.

One evening a month, the shop sponsors meetings for ABUSE (Associated Butlers Under Service to the families of Eel-Smack and Environs), at which members present papers and give lectures on matters close to the domestic's heart, such as the effectiveness of waxing against the grain of wood rather than with it.

I myself have never been invited to speak. I am sure I do not know why this should be so, and I certainly was not expecting such an invitation to be forthcoming today. I chose that location as a meeting place simply because I needed to pick up the new suit I was forced to order when I lost two others to the triplets' "art."

Once introductions were over and my new suit paid for, Smithers and I went outside and seated ourselves on the wrought-iron bench in front of the shop. I told him a bit about the family (but just a little, as I did not wish to frighten away the only applicant I have had). He smiled and said that he thought that he could handle it.

After excusing my lack of discretion in the interest of making him familiar with certain things he was likely to encounter, I told him a little more. Including a bit about the time I found banded snapping turtles in the linen closet and how uncomfortable that had been. He actually chuckled.

"Never put your hands where you can't see them, eh, Tristan, old chum?"

I must say that I was a bit put off by his familiar use of my given name. Well, by that and by the somewhat smug expression upon his face. Nonetheless, I shall meet with him again, because as I say, there haven't been any other applicants. I'd also like to be certain he understands the duties expected of him.

When I returned to the Lighthouse on the Hill,
I contacted the company from which I ordered
tropical flower seeds some weeks ago. The
fellow I spoke with claims that they were sent
right away and should certainly have arrived
by now. He agreed to send more at no charge
since it was no doubt his mistake in addressing
the original packet. To reward his graciousness in
Admitting His Error, I ordered hibiscus seeds as
well. As a result of my considerable horticulture
skill, in 3 weeks, 4 days, 2 hours, and 16 minutes,
the garden of my Charming Cottage Far, Far Away
will be on its way to becoming a tropical paradise.
This reminds me that I must contact the real-
estate company that was to have sent a brochure
advertising Charming Cottages in Warm Climates
Far, Far Away. I fear it a sign of societal decay that
no one seems capable of correctly addressing
mail these days.

My book project continues, though the publisher I am dealing with refuses to advance me
any money. After reading the pages I have sent

so far, including a recent addition about Heyboy, the editor fears my demise before I am able to finish. It is rather nice to know that <u>someone</u> recognizes the perils of my close association with this family.

· 11 ·

A FAMILY DISCUSSION

A few days later, the Bellweathers sat in the third-floor dining room enjoying a bit of lamb, but just a bit. Somehow, in spite of Benway's careful marketing, and the increase of food in the house, Heygirl had taken it upon herself to relieve the family of most of their dinner. She seemed a bit temperamental these days, and no one dared disturb her when she was nosing around the kitchen.

Spider was earnestly trying to figure out a different location for an Endangered Albino Alligator Reserve. He had decided that he couldn't move Heygirl right now, but he intended to do so as soon as the eggs hatched. He kept looking for opportunities to slip this into the conversation within Benway's hearing. This way he figured Benway would know that life in the Lighthouse on the Hill was soon to be more comfortable.

Dinner was turning out to be a typically loud one. In the past, the volume of the family during mealtimes had provided a perfect distraction for any number of Ninda's "guests" to escape. The Balboas, imprisoned in Ninda's room, were unaware of this and so did not take advantage of the opportunity.

"I can't seem to find anything on the incubation period of the Endangered Albino Alligator," Spider said, helping himself to more salad. He was leaving as much lamb as possible for Dr. Bellweather. The professor's sense of humor was more easily engaged when he wasn't well fed.

"I'd like to be able to have some ballpark idea of when the hatchlings can be expected."

"WHY SHOULD IT MATTER?" screamed Sassy, pouring molasses onto her plate. At a nod from

Spike and Brick, she continued her drizzle over the tablecloth, and onto their plates. The intended target of the molasses seemed to be the triplets' portions of broccoli. Benway left the dining room to retrieve a sponge.

"WON'T THEY HATCH WHEN THEY HATCH?" shouted Brick.

"I need to prepare for them," Spider answered.

"Preparations such as building sturdy pens for them to be locked up in?" Eugene Bellweather asked. He was always complaining of being snapped at whenever he left his laboratory and had accused Spider of not caring that this was so.

"Of course not," Spider said, stalling because Benway had left the room. He needed to make sure Benway heard of his plan to find a new home for Heygirl. "It's not a good idea to cage animals when you're trying to study their habits. It interferes with their natural cycles and movement patterns."

"It may not be a good idea to cage animals, but it's a *terrible* idea to have five Endangered Albino Alligators running about the house," Dr. Bellweather said.

His busy eyebrows started to wake up. "Particularly once the hatchlings grow to the size of their mother."

"POOR DADDY DOESN'T LIKE ITTY-BITTY ALLIGATORS." The triplets smirked.

Dr. Bellweather ignored them and instead glowered at his lambless plate. "Is there any more meat in the kitchen?" he asked. His eyes scanned the table, as if looking for something to throw in order to lighten the mood in his jovial manner. His eyebrows yawned and stretched. He turned to his wife. "Can't you do something?" he demanded. Lillian Bellweather turned her beautiful eyes on her oldest child.

"Darling, you know I adore Heygirl," she said in her sweet voice. "But she is awfully hard on the walls. Her tail smears the paint terribly. Of course, I don't mind touching up after her, but it may be difficult to do that with four more alligators about."

Spider, his mouth full of broccoli, nodded his head with vigor, hoping to indicate his agreement with his mother that the Lighthouse on the Hill was no suitable place for an Endangered Albino Alligator Nursery.

"Well, it's settled," Dr. Bellweather said. "I'll call the zoo first thing in the morning."

"THAT WON'T WORK!" screamed Brick.

"SPIDER NEEDS TO STUDY THE BABIES!" shouted Spike.

"SO HE CAN FIGURE OUT HOW TO KEEP THEM FROM STINKING!" yelled Sassy.

"Becoming extinct," Spider corrected, swallowing his broccoli. Benway reentered the dining room and started sponging at the molasses on the table. Spider nodded to his younger siblings.

"You're right about the zoo," he said. "What's *really* needed is an Endangered Albino Alligator Habitat." Spider glanced at Benway, trying to gauge his reaction. He didn't notice Dr. Bellweather, whose eyebrows were beginning their calisthenics. "I know Heygirl makes Benway uncomfortable, and as soon as I find a place and am able to properly establish an environment favorable to—"

Dr. Bellweather made a grab for the milk pitcher. Spider looked over at him. The professor's eyebrows started to dance what looked like the watusi.

"Makes Benway uncomfortable? Benway?!" he roared.

"Soon," Spider said, with a last glance at Benway before ducking, "I'll find a place for them *soon*!"

⸺⸻⸺

August 11,
GLOAT minus 3 weeks, 2 hours, and 22 minutes

Dear Journal,

We were treated to a demonstration of Dr. Bellweather's peculiar sense of humor tonight. I don't know if I'm more grateful for the fact that I was not the target, or that it appears I'll not always have to wear steel-toed boots just to dust Spider's lair. I'm not one to complain, but it seems to me that the tiny nibbles of baby alligators, while not as Potentially Amputating as those of an adult, would be Quite Painful.

Surprisingly, Spider implied that concern for my comfort was a motive in his efforts to

relocate that lumbering brute and her hatchlings.
I am wondering, however, where Spider can
possibly find a habitat. Eel-Smack-by-the-Bay
and its surroundings hardly seem suitable, and
I am filled with yet another unpleasant sense of
foreboding. . . .

Nevertheless, it does seem possible that Heygirl will no longer be in residence by the time
the Wretched Oath of Fealty is fulfilled and my
replacement is installed in the Lighthouse on
the Hill. No Heygirl. How convenient for him.
He may never know the trouble of running a
household with an Endangered Albino Alligator
as a member. Such a callow youth will have no
notion of his luck.

Ah well, I find it easy enough to put envy
behind me in light of the pleasant surprise I had
today. It was while on my daily constitutional to
the village that I bumped into Eli Isbn, of Isbn's
Book Shoppe. He is a thoroughly pleasant fellow.

I mentioned my book-writing venture to
him, and the good man was Most Enthusiastic.

He offered to throw a party at his store when the tome is released, so that I may sign copies for the inhabitants of the village.

I expressed the notion that perhaps no one would show up.

"Nonsense, Tristan, old chap," he said, clapping me on the shoulder. "I'll advertise it well, and I'll bet you the whole village will turn out to hear you read from it!"

The honor of having received such an invitation is something I'll enjoy looking back upon after my departure, a mere 3 weeks, 2 hours, and 19 minutes from now!

Perhaps Smithers won't have to put up with Endangered Albino Alligators, but I'll wager he's never had the prospect of an entire village turning out to hear him read, either!

Fancy that!

AN EXPEDITION IS OUTFITTED
·12·

During the second week in August, Spike, Sassy, and Brick left the Lighthouse on the Hill bright and early one morning, carrying the bag lunches that Benway had prepared for them. They breathed in the fresh, outside air with deep satisfaction. It was good to get outside. For some reason, lately there had been an overpoweringly unpleasant odor mingling with the usual smell of fresh paint inside the lighthouse. It was particularly strong just outside of Ninda's room.

The three were on a mission, and Up to No Good.

They walked along in the thin sunlight, whispering. The hair on the necks of every living thing within a five-mile radius stood on end.

Spike examined the contents of his paper bag. He smiled. There was a container of Brussels sprouts and a packet of boysenberry jam, his favorite.

"Are you thinking what I'm thinking?" Spike asked the others.

"If you're thinking that we need to Come Up with Something to Keep Benway, then I'm thinking what you're thinking," Sassy whispered. She had just peeked into her own lunch bag and was happy to discover that it contained green beans and marshmallows.

"If you're thinking that Benway would like something Grand and Fine, then I'm thinking what you're thinking," Brick whispered after examining his lunch bag, too. The sight of pickled beets and chocolate syrup was a beautiful one.

Benway may mutter under his breath about their taste in food, but he could always be counted upon to give them what they liked, and they'd always appreciated that. Not that they'd ever told him so.

"If you're thinking that the *Mona Lisa* is Grand and Fine, then I'm thinking what you're thinking," Sassy whispered.

"If you are thinking that if instead of just hiding the Grand and Fine *Mona Lisa*, we should take it and give it to Benway, then I am thinking what you are thinking," Brick told his siblings.

"If I'm thinking that we should *not* let Spider and Ninda know what we're thinking, then I'm thinking what I'm thinking, too," said Spike.

And so it was that the triplets decided they would steal the *Mona Lisa* and present it to Benway. Of course, they did not consider themselves common thieves. No, they referred to the proposed theft as Anonymously Borrowing the painting, and compared themselves to Robin Hood.

"After all," they reasoned, "France is rich and Benway is poor—that's why he has to work. If France were poor, it would be our butler and we'd have to eat snails without the ice cream. We're just Anonymously Borrowing from the rich and giving to the poor."

When they got to the museum, they sat on its steps and waited for it to open. The triplets had become a fixture there, falling into a routine of leaving the Lighthouse on the Hill early in the morning and not returning until well after the building had closed for the night.

Eel-Smack-by-the-Bay has a rather good-sized museum for a village of its population. There are three wings to the building. The first of these holds fine-art exhibits. The triplets, no strangers to this area, had previously enjoyed many an hour there, usually when they felt themselves artistically blocked.

A second wing of the museum houses a natural-history exhibit. This exhibit is filled with stuffed saber-toothed tigers, fierce-looking warthogs, and stubby cavemen who hunch in front of a gray Styrofoam cave and grind meal on a stone slab, while a little baby on a cradle board looks on in a most life-like manner. The triplets loved to walk through the natural-history exhibit and talk about how many cavemen could be eaten by a stuffed tiger.

The third wing houses a planetarium. At the time

of the Global Art Exchange, Eel-Smack's museum was hosting an exhibit depicting the Big Bang. The triplets shivered in ecstasy every time they chanced past it, which they managed to do several times a visit. "Just *think* of the noise!" Spike whispered to his siblings.

The triplets haunted all three of the areas. They admired the art and debated the wisdom of perhaps Anonymously Borrowing some of the other pieces. They enjoyed opening doors marked KEEP OUT and AUTHORIZED PERSONNEL ONLY. Still, they were careful to stay out of trouble. Naturally, being Up to No Good, they spoke in the dreaded whisper, unless the curator of the museum were nearby. He passed by them several times a day without suspicion due to their deceptively innocent blue eyes and hushed voices.

They watched and waited and waited and watched. They observed the habits of the museum guards. There were two, and their shifts just overlapped. The daytime guard was a very skinny man. He mostly hung around the front door, coming away from it only toward the end of the day to call out, "Thirty minutes to closing," then, "Twenty minutes to closing," then, "Ten minutes to closing," in a reedy voice. The triplets took to calling him "Whippet," because he resembled that very thin breed of dog.

The other guard was a huge man with a floppy mustache that waggled when he breathed in and out. He came in toward the end of the day and stayed at the museum after it closed for the night. The triplets called him "Walrus." He walked around the museum every hour or so and spent the rest of the time near the natural history wing, shut away behind a door marked AUTHORIZED PERSONNEL ONLY.

After a few days of "casing the joint," as Spike liked to say, the triplets began to bring little bits and pieces of things they thought they'd need in order to pull off the caper. When no one was looking, they hid these behind the Styrofoam cave in the natural-history wing. Their masterpiece had been rolled up inside of a cardboard canister similar to the ones the museum gift shop used to protect the art posters it sold. Sassy brought the panther costumes they'd worn the previous Halloween, and snacks for the long night they planned to spend inside the locked museum. Spike brought an old quilt to wrap around the *Mona Lisa* to keep it from getting damaged. Finally, Brick brought grappling hooks.

The triplets knew they had no real use for the hooks; however, they agreed amongst themselves that rappelling down the walls of the museum would be a mighty fine thing, should the opportunity to do so arise.

———⋙●⋘———

August 17,
GLOAT minus 2 weeks, 1 day, 2 hours, and 22 minutes

Dear Journal,

I experienced a most unsatisfactory meeting with Smithers today. I had been in a thoroughly excellent mood, having just passed by Isbn's

Book Shoppe. True to his word, Isbn had placed a strikingly well-designed advertisement for my book-signing party in the window of his establishment. It was a gratifying sight to me. I was unprepared, however, for the sight that greeted me when I arrived at Tuxedos and Ice Cream.

Wodehouse Smithers was modeling the very latest in formal wear (a suit I had tried on, but deemed too extravagant for my budget). He was eating an ice-cream cone! I could hardly caution a grown man about such an infantile action—instead I addressed the issue of clothing itself. I complimented him on the cut—then warned him that should he choose to purchase the suit, he should not become too attached to it. I told him a little bit about the triplets (but just a little, as I did not wish to frighten him away). He smiled his smug smile.

"How difficult could three nine-year-olds be?" he asked.

So I told him a little more, including a bit about them turning two of my best suits into "art."

It isn't in the nature of those who choose my profession to guffaw. It speaks volumes to me that this is precisely what Wodehouse Smithers did. He guffawed.

"Sounds like you needed to take a firmer hand with them, and they knew it. I shall expect good behavior from them, and they will live up to my expectations. It's all in the attitude, old bean."

The ice cream began to look a little melty.

"At any rate, I don't intend to wear this suit when I serve the family," he said. "I shall wear it at the October meeting of ABUSE. I've been invited to speak."

It is a good thing that it was not I who was indulging in ice cream. I might have choked. "What in the world will you be speaking about?" I managed to ask.

"Oh, there're any number of topics to choose from," he said.

"From which to choose," I corrected, observing the chocolate drip onto one of his cuffs. I did not point this out to him. Instead I mentioned an appointment I had forgotten and promised to meet with him another time.

Speaking at the October meeting of ABUSE, indeed! It is not that I envy such an invitation— I just wonder what in the world a youthful new- comer to the profession could have to offer his well-established and more experienced elders.

I am exceedingly grateful that this sure-to-be Unhelpful lecture is to take place <u>after</u> my Glori- ous Liberation 2 weeks, 1 day, 2 hours, and 19 minutes from now!

·13·
THE BALBOAS EXPERIENCE AN UNWELCOME ENCOUNTER

Ninda left the hardware store, kerosene for Igor's fire-eating practice tucked into the string bag she carried over her shoulder. The bag was already heavy with a cantaloupe, some morning buns, and the usual cans of tuna. Professor Bellweather would be less likely to unleash his sense of humor on Benway if the larder of the Lighthouse on the Hill were full of food.

Glancing down at the pamphlet "From Silkworms to Honeybees: Unionization for ALL Creatures," she considered reading it out loud to the circus perform-ers after lunch. Maybe it would be the thing that helped the family to score higher than the dismal 57% they had collectively received on the practice test she'd administered the day before.

She stopped in at Isbn's Book Shoppe to pick up an English/Rhinnestadtian dictionary. Maybe the language barrier was the problem. Once she could converse with the Balboas in their native language, things would surely go more smoothly. She left the Book Shoppe and was almost past the plate-glass window when she stopped dead.

Staring out at her from a poster hanging in the window in a most unfamiliar way was the *very* familiar face of Benway. She stepped closer to read the advertisement printed at the bottom.

It said, **Come hear local author, Tristan Benway, butler to Eel-Smack's most notorious family, read from his new book.**

Benway had written a book???!!!

What could he have possibly written a book *about*?

She had heard that writers should write about what they know . . . perhaps it was a book about house-cleaning? Or maybe tips for gardening? He used to garden quite enthusiastically, but come to think of it, she hadn't noticed him doing that lately—not since there were so many holes around the garden and front yard, anyway.

Benway had never mentioned the book to the family. If she were to write a book, she'd stop people in the street to tell them and to make sure she got credit for it.

Shoving the new dictionary into her string bag, she hurried the rest of the way to the Lighthouse on the Hill.

She had inquired of Benway if he was feeling Downtrodden, and she had inquired of him if he was feeling Exploited. She had never thought to inquire of him if he was Writing a Book! And how strange that he had a life she knew nothing about!

Ninda charged up the lighthouse steps and pushed open the door. Suddenly she had lots of questions to ask him.

"Benway?!" she shouted, heading upstairs.

She found him on the staircase outside his third-floor quarters.

"Yes?" he asked, eyes on his task. He was scraping eggshells and candle wax off the floor.

Standing there watching him work, Ninda was suddenly flustered. What if she wasn't meant to know about the book?

"Um ... are you feeling Downtrodden?" she asked.

He looked up at her.

"Are you feeling Exploited?"

"Why do you ask?" he finally said.

Surely Benway had no secrets from the family.

"What's your book about?"

"My book?!" Benway sounded surprised.

"Yes, your book. Is it about housekeeping?"

"You might say that," he conceded, an odd expression on his face.

"Oh, but that's wonderful! Lighthousehold hints!"

Before Benway could elaborate, a thundering white streak barreled up the steps behind Ninda. Heygirl, teeth clacking, tornadoed upstairs toward Ninda's bedroom.

"The Balboas!" she shouted, ditching Benway and running after the gator.

The gagging stench of days old anchovies and wet seal hit hard when she got close to her room. Some of the joy had definitely gone out of suffering for this cause.

THUMP...BASH...CRASH. When she turned the curve to the landing outside of her room, all thoughts of Benway's book fled. Before Ninda's bedroom stood Heygirl. The gator had a most malevolent gleam in her eyes as she bashed at the closed door with her snout. She had obviously followed her nose to the source of the most delicious stench imaginable (to an alligator), the rotting-fish odor of Elza the trained seal.

Ninda rolled up her pamphlet and used it to gently thwack Heygirl on the nose. The bashing and teeth snapping were probably making the Balboas too nervous to study.

"Shoo!" she said. Heygirl didn't shoo.

"Bad girl! Go away!" Ninda scolded. Heygirl didn't budge.

"I"–*thwack*–"said"–*thwack*–"go"–*thwack*–"away." *Thwack.*

The alligator finally hung her head and moved off down the hall. Ninda came in and shut the door.

She took in the frightened expressions on the faces of her prisone– ahem, guests, noting that the coiled tightrope, Elza's red ball with the gold stars, and Igor's fire-eating equipment were packed together as if in readiness to go.

"Sorry about that," Ninda said. "She's mostly harmless, especially if you don't try to leave this room."

Truly, unless they passed their test, the Balboas would have to resort to drastic action in order to leave. Ninda smiled to herself. And what could possibly be considered drastic in this household?

⟫●⟪

August 21,
GLOAT minus 1 week, 4 days, 3 hours, and 49 minutes

Dear Journal,
   Other than a little Heygirl incident today,

the Lighthouse on the Hill has been (relatively) quiet. Spider has assured me that he is engaged in a hunt for a new habitat for Heygirl and her offspring and again implied that he was doing so out of concern for _my_ comfort! Imagine that, Dear Journal! I hardly knew what to say, and so I simply went about mopping the hall outside of Ninda's bedroom. There was Heygirl saliva all over the floor.

Ninda paid me a visit today, but it was interrupted by that beast. It was the first time in a very long time she stopped by my quarters to inquire as to whether I was feeling Downtrodden or Exploited. Not that I miss her visits, of course. It is just something that I have noticed.

The biggest reason for the (relative) quiet in the Lighthouse on the Hill is that the triplets are engaged in activity elsewhere. I admit to breathing a bit easier knowing that none of the objects of my responsibility are present targets for those hellions. Still I can't help but wonder what they've gotten up to. I know I shall find

out soon enough—I always do . . . but perhaps
I ought to follow them on my next day off. I'm
certain that Smithers will never use his free time
just to check up on the family . . . the trouble
with so many of this new generation of servants
is that there's no loyalty to the families they
serve.

This unexpected (relative) quiet in the Lighthouse on the Hill has caused me to reflect a bit
on how quiet my Charming Cottage Far, Far Away
will be. I am afraid I shall have to locate one after
I have fulfilled my Glorious Oath to leave this
family. The catalog never did arrive!

I may not know exactly where my new home
is to be located, but I do know one thing about it.
It will be Quiet. And therefore Blissful.

And yet . . . and yet . . . perhaps I will look into
purchasing a companion pet. Certainly nothing
like an Endangered Albino Alligator. Perhaps a
budgie, or if I am feeling very exotic, a parrot.
Just a creature to provide me with a tiny, low
level of background noise. One which will Keep

Me Company perhaps. Not that I will be lonely.
As I've said—I quite look forward to the Quiet
and Solitude I am to enjoy in 1 week, 4 days,
3 hours, and 46 minutes.

Truly.

·14·

THE LADY SMILES,
THE TRIPLETS GRIN, AND THE
BELLWEATHERS ATTEND CHURCH

As usual, the triplets were up bright and early on Sunday. The big day had arrived, and the Global Art Exchange was finally opening. The triplets planned to go see it before church. The steps of the museum were so crowded that were they ordinary nine-year-olds, they would have had difficulty pushing their way up to the entrance. Of course they were first in line when the doors opened at 8:00 A.M. There was a woman from the news-paper taking pictures. With her was a reporter who asked everyone stupid questions about whether they were excited to see such great works of art.

"JUST WHAT DOES HE THINK ALL THESE PEOPLE ARE DOING HERE IF THEY AREN'T EXCITED?" screamed Sassy.

The crowd surged into the building and over to the fine-art wing with the triplets leading the charge. They stopped short when they saw that a temporary barrier separated that area of the museum. The curator stood next to it. "Ten at a time, only ten at a time," she called. The triplets, of course, pushed their way into being among the first ten who would be allowed to view the painting up close. They weren't particularly anxious to see it; after all, it would soon be in their possession. They just liked being first for everything.

The curator led the small group down a corridor to a large room, which would have accommodated far more than ten. On the way she lectured the group about Leonardo da Vinci, the times he lived in, and the fact that he was also an inventor.

"I bet he could have invented a really clever way to anonymously add his painting to a museum," Spike whispered to Sassy and Brick. They snickered quietly, being Up to No Good.

The curator stopped in front of a very fine-looking red velvet rope, which was all that separated the painting from the viewers. Upon first glance, the triplets were transfixed. The merest hint of a smile played across the lady's lips, and the rich colors of the portrait evoked a bygone era. Artists themselves, they appreciated mastery when they saw it, and here was mastery. Others in the group oohed and ahhhed.

"It'll look great in Benway's room," Brick finally whispered. The other two nodded, not taking their eyes off the masterpiece. Of course, the main task was still aimed at gaining attention for their own masterpiece . . . but on their way to church, they made plans to smuggle another quilt into the museum for the further protection of the *Mona Lisa*.

The Bellweathers regularly attend church. Every Sunday one can find them at Our Lady of the Benevolent Soup. Their reasons for attending are varied.

Eugene Bellweather attends services because the

tremulous but droning voice of the Reverend Shrift—
a short man—induces in him a half-dream state. Dr.
Bellweather has found this state to be helpful to
inspiration for new inventions.

Lillian Bellweather attends services because it gives
the paint a chance to dry.

Spider attends services because his hero, Galileo,
discovered the Law of the Pendulum* while watching a chandelier swing during a church service in
Pisa. Spider was ever on the lookout for a scientific
discovery of his own.

Ninda attends services because Our Lady of the
Benevolent Soup sponsors several programs benefit-
ing the poor and downtrodden.

The triplets attend services because they find many
opportunities for mischief there.

The Bellweather family sat in their usual pew at
the very back of the church. They always chose that

---

*The Law of the Pendulum simply stated that each swing of the chandelier
took the same amount of time, even though the arc of each swing was
shorter than the previous one. This may seem ho-hum now . . . but back
then, it was a big deal. Computer games hadn't been invented yet, so people
had less to think about and were more easily impressed.

pew because Eugene's occasional snores weren't so obvious from there. Also, the triplets could easily slip out to investigate anything they deemed worthy of investigation.

The Reverend Shrift began his trembling drone up at the front of the church. He was a nervous man who startled easily. Thunderstorms, fast drivers, large animals, and loud noises were just a few of the things that caused him great discomfort.

He was very glad that the Bellweather family chose to sit at the back of the church very far away from him.

Eugene snored lightly as Lillian gazed longingly at the walls of the chapel, imagining them a beautiful chartreuse.

Spider stared off into space and worried about finding a place to establish the world's first Endangered Albino Alligator Habitat. The eggs had hatched three days ago. The hatchlings were cute, but Benway had been Most Unenthusiastic about their arrival. Also, it seemed to Spider that Heygirl was looking harried and cramped in the bathtub with her babies.

Next to Spider sat Ninda, who was wondering

how to say certain words in Rhinnestaadtian. For the most part she was satisfied that her language learning was going so well. She knew the words for *exploit* (*exploitatzek*), *struggle* (*struglek*), and *suffer* (*sufbek*). She was a bit frustrated to realize she'd left her English/Rhinnestaadtian grammar book at home. It would have been nice to look up the words for *protest* and *complain*. She reflected sadly that the Balboa family seemed just as disinclined to complain or protest in their native tongue as they were in English.

From underneath the chapel floor came a faint but insistent clanking noise. Spike heard it first. He glanced over at Sassy to see if she heard it as well. Her eyes met his; she smiled, and then nudged Brick. The triplets loved nothing better than a good distraction during church. The clanking continued.

"Let's go," whispered Brick, confirming that he was Up to No Good. They all squeezed past Spider and Ninda.

"Where are you guys going?" Ninda asked. She wasn't all that keen on the Reverend's sermons, and she'd heard this particular one more than a few times before. In fact, the entire congregation had.

When the subject of the sermon was "Thou Shalt Not Steal," church members knew that someone had broken in and robbed the collection plates again. This was not an uncommon occurrence, but the Reverend Shrift (whom Dr. Bellweather liked to say was short on brains as well as in stature), could never figure out how the thieves had gotten in, nor could he spare the money to hire a night watchman for the building. Guarding the church himself was, for obvious reasons, out of the question.

"There's a noise," Sassy whispered to Ninda, as if that explained everything. Ninda nodded.

"I'll come, too," she said, then turned to Spider. "You?" she asked.

Spider shrugged his shoulders, then stood and followed the paint-smeared backs of his siblings out past the church lobby.

"I think the noise was coming from the basement," Spike whispered.

"It's just the plumbing," Spider informed them, but

he made no move to turn back when they opened a door off the lobby. The door itself was marked DO NOT ENTER. Of course, what lay beyond it was familiar to the triplets, who knew that the phrase "Do not enter" as well as the words "Keep out" and "No admittance" were code for "Come on in, Spike, Sassy, and Brick!"

Beyond the door there were two staircases. One led up to the organ loft, where the enormous pipes of the church organ were housed. The pipes amplified any noise that was shrieked into them. The triplets, the congregation, and the Reverend Shrift discovered that information simultaneously one day, in a heart-stopping, earsplitting fashion. The Reverend had spent the following week in bed.

The other staircase led down to the basement of the church. It was this staircase that the Bellweather children took.

The basement of the church contains sublevel meeting rooms connected by a series of hallways. The windows are few and high, thereby letting in very little natural light, just as Spider likes them to be. The air is dank and musty, just as Spider likes air to be. Most of the church's members, however, do not share Spider's tastes. When the community center was built across the parking lot from the chapel, the rooms fell into disuse.

Spider pulled out his flashlight and led his siblings to the disappointingly dull source of the clanging.

"See?" he said, reaching up and knocking one of the exposed pipes. "When water flows through these, they change temperature and the metal expands and contracts. That's what makes the clanging noise you hear."

"BORING," screamed Sassy.

"You're right," Spider agreed.

"WHO SPIT ON ME?" Brick suddenly flailed at his siblings.

Spider quickly shined his flashlight above Brick's head. "Calm down," he said. "They're just a little leaky."

Brick glanced at Sassy and Spike with suspicion while Spider allowed the flashlight beam to play over the surface of the pipes. "Very leaky," he amended. They fairly glistened as water beaded out of them.

"Hmmm," he said as he began moving down the corridor. His brothers and sisters trailed after him. He continued to shine his flashlight along the plumbing. Despite the darkness of the basement, a light had dawned on Spider Bellweather.

"These are some old pipes," he said. "Yes, indeed. Some old and drippy pipes." The other children nodded; they knew that *something* was coming. "So old and drippy that they'd need very little encouragement to burst."

Ninda was shocked. "*They're* the destructive ones," she said, gesturing to the triplets. "Not you."

"Thereby flooding this basement and providing an ideal habitat for Endangered Albino Alligators," he explained, in a superior tone. He turned to the triplets. "You three can help me," he said.

"Yippee!" the triplets cheered in a whisper, being Up to No Good.

And so it was that Spider decided upon the perfect place for an Endangered Albino Alligator Habitat. It was the basement of the Reverend Shrift's church. Surely Benway would appreciate the gesture.

August 23,
GLOAT minus 1 week, 2 days, 4 hours, and 4
minutes

Dear Journal,

I chose the sidewalk out in front of Isbn's Book
Shoppe as a place to meet with Smithers today.
I'm afraid I was a little tardy. When I arrived, he
was studying the various signage in the window.
Imagine! I had Quite Forgotten about the notice
of my book-signing party that Isbn had so
kindly placed there. I am hopeful it didn't make
Smithers's invitation to speak at ABUSE pale in
comparison. Before Smithers could say anything,
I suggested we take our constitutional.

As we strolled, I told him a little bit about
Ninda (but just a little bit, as he was still the only
applicant).

"She doesn't sound so bad," he said.

So I told him some more, including a bit about

having to shoo a couple of vagrants out of my
bed.

He chuckled in that know-it-all way of his.
"Sounds as though you should have kept your
door locked, old chap! Perhaps I'll choose privacy issues as the topic for my speech at the
October meeting of ABUSE."

I am not at all certain that Smithers is the right
fellow for the job.

I have qualms about leaving the Bellweathers
in the care of such an odious know-it-all. Yet
as they say, my hands are tied. He was the only
fellow to apply for the position. It is unthink-
able that I should leave the family without help,
and even if I dared to stay around long enough
to find a more suitable replacement once my
book is published, I could not. I have vowed to
leave the Bellweather family just as surely as my
ancestor vowed to serve them. A hallmark of the
Benway family is that we are men of our word.
This has ever been our tragedy.

I do find myself wondering if Ninda will visit

Smithers to ask if he's feeling Downtrodden or
Exploited—and whether Spider will offer to
relocate any of the dangerous pets he is sure to
continue to bring into the Lighthouse on the Hill.

I wonder, too, what Smithers would do if
he were the one to discover an entire family of
circus performers and their pet seal living in
Ninda's bedroom. I must say, I find my concern
growing for that poor family . . . I should think
that such crowded conditions would be tiresome.
I wonder why they don't leave?

I overheard the triplets whispering today.
Once I had managed to get the hair on the back
of my neck to lie down again, I checked on
the neighborhood dogs. They are all accounted
for. But what will become of them after I have
gone—1 week, 2 days, 4 hours, and 1 minute
from now?

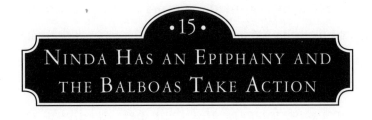

· 15 ·
NINDA HAS AN EPIPHANY AND THE BALBOAS TAKE ACTION

Monday afternoon Ninda climbed down the dunes on the ocean side of the lighthouse. She was anxious to get her bagpipe practice out of the way early, since she planned to help move Heygirl and the baby gators to their new home that night.

No doubt that would improve Benway's frame of mind.

Ninda found her favorite spot, took a deep breath, and raised the chanter to her lips. She began her warm-ups and allowed her mind to wander.

She wondered again about Benway's book. Beneath

his professional exterior she could sense his discomfort whenever she brought it up. Clearly he was a modest man—and there was much about him that the Bellweathers did not know.

It bothered her to think that Benway was only with the family out of a sense of duty. It bothered her, too, that he was clearly suffering under the delusion that he was an indentured servant of some sort. To think that someone in this day and age, someone so close to her could be so uneducated about his rights as a human being . . . She set down her bagpipes to zip up the sweatshirt Benway insisted she put on just before she left the lighthouse. A realization came to her so suddenly that she nearly kicked her instrument over.

Charity begins at home! Or it should, anyway. How terrible that she should spend all her time and resources on the obstinate and ungrateful Balboas when Benway needed her so! Her clear blue eyes narrowed and darkened, this time at her own injustice.

The Balboas would just have to leave even though none had ever scored above 61% on the practice tests.

Benway was her priority—as he should have been.

Hopefully the Balboas had absorbed enough information under her tutelage to recognize their rights as human beings and workers. If not, well . . . not belonging to a union significantly paled in comparison to indentured servitude!

Scooping up her bagpipes, Ninda started back toward home. She needed to set things right immediately. She looked up at the lighthouse and was startled to see smoke billowing from *her* bedroom window. She scrambled up the dune and began to run. At the front door, she collided with Balfour Justice. He'd seen the smoke, too.

"Do you know if anyone's in there?" the lawyer asked, once he'd disentangled himself from the drones of the bagpipe.

Lillian and Spider were in Shelbywood picking up paint. The triplets had gone off to the museum and, as far as Ninda knew, had not yet returned. Benway had departed the lighthouse when she had, which left only . . . "Dad and the Balboas!" she cried before running into the house. (Later she was made aware that this was very, very wrong . . . one must run *out* of a building one suspects to be on fire, not *into* it.)

"FIRE!" she shouted. "FIRE!" Mr. Justice followed and grabbed her before she could run up the stairs. She shook him off.

"My father can't hear me from here! And there's a family of circus performers and their trained seal in my bedroom!"

He held on to her. "I already called the fire department," he said. "We need to wait outside."

Ninda couldn't be budged, so he grabbed her bagpipes and tried to use them to drag her out of the Lighthouse on the Hill. She got her mouth onto the chanter and gave it a blast. From somewhere up above a door slammed open.

"No more noise!" roared Dr. Bellweather.

Another door slammed open. The sound of excited voices, a barking seal, and feet thumping on stairs filled the air.

"Who are you?" At Dr. Bellweather's shout there was a brief silence during which an approaching siren could be heard. "And why do I smell smoke?"

The cacophony of sound in the stairwell resumed with the addition of heavy foot stomps that could only belong to Dr. Bellweather.

Ninda saw Elza first, who was loping toward the front door at a remarkable speed for a pinniped. Pim, Anya, and Igor were close behind, with Igor lugging the bag containing his family's possessions. Viktor Balboa and Dr. Bellweather shepherded everyone out to the front lawn, just as the Eel-Smack Volunteer Fire Department pulled up to the Lighthouse on the Hill. (Ninda later heard a rumor that there was a discussion among some of its members about whether the VFD should have responded to a fire in *that* location so quickly.)

Firemen jumped out of the truck and began uncoiling hoses. Ninda, Dr. Bellweather, and Mr. Justice turned to look up at the billowing smoke.

"What happened?" Mr. Justice asked.

"I don't know, I . . ." Ninda looked around her for the Balboas. They were inching off behind the fire truck. "My guests are getting away!"

Balfour Justice went charging after them. "Whoa,

wait." The family kept moving. "Stop right there!" he shouted.

The Balboas stopped. This must be the Corrupt Immigration Official that Ninda had so often warned them about. There would be no escaping him.

The firemen trained their hoses on Ninda's window. Dr. Bellweather's eyebrows skipped their warm-up and went straight into their frenzied routine.

"Do you see what comes of harboring vagrants against your poor, overworked father's wishes?" he shouted at Ninda.

The Balboas shrank back.

"I'm sure they didn't mean to set the house on fire," Ninda told her father. She turned to the Balboas. "Did you?"

There was a slight hesitation before Viktor answered. He had finally discovered what *could* be considered drastic in the Bellweathers' strange household. He looked from Ninda to Mr. Justice to the towering, raging Dr. Bellweather, whose leaping eyebrows were mesmerizing in a terrifying sort of way.

"Igor just practicing was. Window coverings flamed up, poof!"

"See?" Ninda asked her father. "Igor breathes fire in their act. They're not vagrants, they're circus performers."

"More friends of yours, Ninda?" Balfour Justice had become acquainted with some of Ninda's friends in the past, even representing a few of them in the occasional labor dispute.

The professor turned to the lawyer. He gave an exaggerated nod. "Oh, excuse me, Balfour—I'm sure you came by to see how your window-washing invention was coming along. Unfortunately, it's not done, because I keep getting interrupted by the little things, you know." His eyebrows performed dual jackknifes. "Tiny little things like Endangered Albino Alligators, forbidden bagpipe playing, *and a daughter who brings in hobos to set my house on fire!*" His eyebrows arched up again, and then did twin barrel rolls.

"They aren't hobos," Ninda countered. "And my bagpipes probably saved your life! If you hadn't come running out to yell at me, you never would have smelled the fire."

"I NEVER YELL!" Dr. Bellweather shouted.

Ninda and her father forged ahead in their argument. Smoke from the window was already turning from black to gray. The fire had come under control in a remarkably short period of time. Of course, this went unobserved by the two of them. After all, what was a house on fire compared to a Bellweather argument?

The attorney and the Balboas looked at one another. It is always an uncomfortable thing to witness a family squabble.

"So, have you been in this country long?" Mr. Justice asked, by way of small talk. He had to speak loudly in order to be heard over Dr. Bellweather's voice.

"Not so long," answered Viktor. "We come with the Marvolo Circus. We have the paperworks that say we can be here," he added.

"Sounds good," Mr. Justice nodded. "And how long do you plan to stay?"

Viktor and Anya exchanged glances at this trick question. The time to bribe the Corrupt Immigration Official had come.

"Money we have." Viktor dug into the bag Igor carried, withdrew some banknotes, and handed them over.

Mr. Justice was surprised. "Why are you giving me this?" he asked.

"In this country we want to stay," Viktor said. "Please, take the money and let us go."

"Who do you think I am?" The attorney glanced over at Ninda.

"You are Corrupt Immigration Official," answered Viktor.

"I most certainly am not!" Mr. Justice shoved the money back into Viktor's hands. He glared at Ninda. "I wonder *where* you could have gotten that idea!"

Ninda became aware of the attorney's Very Hard Look.

Dr. Bellweather continued his rant. Words like *orphanage* and *poorhouse* and *sleeping in the gutter* spewed from his mouth until he realized Ninda was no longer listening and had, in fact, turned her back on him. She walked toward the Balboas.

"So, you all have met!" She tried to sound happy about it. "Well, Mr. Justice, the Balboas have been staying with me and—" It was Anya who interrupted her.

"In a room she kept us, with alligator outside of door and guards with chainsaws!"

Ninda affected a chuckle. "Oh, you know those triplets and their little projects," she said to Mr. Justice, then to the Balboas, "The important thing is that you learned all about unionization." At least she hoped they had. "And now you can take that information back to your fellow performers! Good luck, and good-bye!" She tried to shoo them away from Mr. Justice.

The Balboas didn't know if they should make a run for it or not.

Mr. Justice held up his hand. "My car is parked at the bottom of the hill. I think we can all squeeze in if you'd like me to give you a lift anywhere."

"We are not like to trouble you," Viktor Balboa said.

"We must find a way to get to Shelbywood, and is very long journey."

"Nonsense." Mr. Justice gave Ninda another Very Hard Look. "We can be there in twenty minutes. You can tell me *all* about the time you spent in the lighthouse on the way." To Ninda he said only, "I'll be talking to you later, young lady."

Ninda waggled her fingers in a weak good-bye. The Balboas and Elza started down the hill with the attorney.

"Be sure and tell Mr. Justice all the valuable things I taught you about human rights!" she called.

Ninda could hear Anya complaining about her accommodations, the food, and the lectures. This turned into whinging about the rigors of a life in the circus, until the group had moved out of earshot. At the bottom of the hill, only Pim and Elza stopped to look back. Pim waved at Ninda, and Elza gave a short bark, probably to thank Ninda for all the tuna fish.

She returned the wave, but her mind was already elsewhere. What if her plan to help Benway was too little, too late? Self-doubt lasted only an instant.

Benway would be so grateful for her loving attention, of course he would want to stay. She wondered which reading materials would most benefit him in his particular situation. The plan to Do Good and Be Kind to someone so close to her made Ninda feel good.

⸎

August 25,
GLOAT minus 1 week, 8 hours, and 27 minutes

Dear Journal,

I have always assumed that when the Lighthouse on the Hill went up in smoke (as was inevitable) that it would be the triplets who were at the bottom of it. Imagine my surprise that the fire started in Ninda's bedroom! It is fortunate that the flames contained themselves to her curtains and the cushion of the window seat. There was a bit of smoke damage to the walls. Lillian is delighted, as this means that Ninda's bedroom will require new paint.

Dr. Bellweather is in a foul temper. Very unusual, is it not? (Permit me to indulge myself in a little sarcasm.) It seems that Balfour Justice has put the skills of the Balboas to good use. What does one do with tightrope walkers and contortionists? Why, one offers them union jobs washing the windows of the tallest building in Eel-Smack-by-the-Bay, of course. Dr. Bellweather expressed his peculiar sense of humor when he discovered there was no immediate need for the window-washing invention he's been working on for the past month and a half. Oh, the broken crockery.

Such displays really do remind me to be glad my long-term employment with this family is nearly at an end.

My book's publication is coming closer, as is the celebration at Isbn's Book Shoppe.

Ninda has somehow learned of my literary endeavor but labors under the impression that my book is to be a how-to manual for the domestic. I am hopeful that by the time Dr. Bellweather discovers the tell-all nature of the manuscript, I shall be Far, Far Away, and it will be the responsibility of Smithers to sweep up the mess. Ha!

Indeed, it is quite possible that Dr. Bellweather will be halfway through throttling Smithers before he realizes that the person he has in hand (or headlock) is not I! Really, this family takes so little notice of me that they are unlikely to recognize my absence for quite some time after I have gone, 1 week, 8 hours, and 24 minutes from now. This is of no consequence to me, I am sure.

Perhaps I will give Smithers a complimentary copy of my book. How nice for him, to have the luxury of learning my tried and true methods for dealing with this family. I am certain no one handed _me_ what is, in effect, practically a how-to manual—oh no, I had to learn as I went along.

On second thought, I don't believe I will give that chap a copy. I'm sure his struggles with this family will be good for his character.

·16·
A HOME FOR HEYGIRL

It is a very wet sort of thing to have firemen spraying water into a house through a bedroom window . . . or any window at all, for that matter. The early evening was spent in mopping up the mess in Ninda's room. The children all pitched in to help.

"After all, Benway, you shouldn't have to do everything alone," they told him, not once but many times, throughout the task. Benway seemed quite surprised. Evidently, he was catching a cold—his eyes watered a bit and he seemed even more gruff than usual.

Ninda's room was put back in sorts, except for

the paint. Lillian had been very sad to learn that she would have to wait until the walls had completely dried before she could get her hands on them.

When Benway went downstairs, the Bellweather children talked. The Reverend Shrift had left the rectory in order to take a "rest cure" at a spa up the coast from Eel-Smack-by-the-Bay. The children naturally had their opinions as to why the Reverend Shrift needed to take a "rest cure" at the Shady Acres Spa and Sanatorium.

"NERVOUS AS A CAT," cackled Sassy.

"CRAZY AS A LOON," guffawed Brick.

"BUGGY AS A TICK-FILLED MATTRESS WITH LOTS OF SPIDERS AND ANTS AND COCKROACHES AND BEETLES AND LISTENING DEVICES," Spike screamed with laughter at his very own fabulous wit.

Whatever the reason for the Reverend's absence, now would be a perfect time to turn the basement of Our Lady of the Benevolent Soup into a proper Endangered Albino Alligator Habitat. The children just needed to settle on a method for bursting the water pipes. The triplets, being experts in the destructive arts, introduced their best-loved schemes.

"I'm in favor of detonating a small bomb," whispered Sassy. She, Spike, and Brick enjoyed a good shiver; the word *detonate* always did that to them.

"That'd bust them pipes up good," Spike agreed, adopting what he supposed to be the terrible grammar of the hardened criminal.

"We need to make sure the building remains intact," Ninda said.

The triplets regarded her with their deceptively innocent blue eyes. "Why?" asked Brick.

"Heygirl's habitat," Spider reminded them.

"Oh, that's right." They nodded to one another. There was a chorus of "well, sure"s and "oh, of course"s.

"We forgot," they apologized to Spider and Ninda.

The plan that was finally agreed upon was both practical and destructive. They would freeze the plumbing in several places. Expanding ice would burst the pipes but allow the Bellweathers to get out of the basement before the ice melted.

To this end the triplets happily dismantled the garden's weed sprayer, retaining the nozzle and tubing and then melting the tank. The sprayer nozzle was then hooked up to a liquid-nitrogen canister, creating a portable freeze machine.

There was no practical purpose to melting the sprayer tank; the three just enjoyed its destruction. They considered adding it to the piece they planned to exhibit in their own Private Art Exchange.

On the other hand, suppose they kept the tank so that Benway could display it next to the *Mona Lisa* when they Anonymously Borrowed the painting to give to him?

At two A.M., Eel-Smack-by-the-Bay is the very definition of a sleepy little town. . . . In fact, one may call it a sleeping little town. In the darkest hour of the night, Spider led Heygirl out of the house on her leash and Ninda followed with the babies in a picnic hamper. The triplets had almost come to blows over who would get to carry the freezing device, but before any blood was shed, Ninda helped them with the decision to take turns.

Spider knew that Thaddeus Bohack was wont to skulk around Eel-Smack-by-the-Bay at all hours of the night. The officer enjoyed rounding up barking dogs and loose cats in the middle of the night while their owners slept. He thought it great fun to listen to them (the owners of the animals, not the creatures themselves) beg for the release of Fluffy or Spot in the morning. It always started his day out right.

It was easy to conceal the baby gators in a picnic hamper. Then Spider rummaged around until he found an old pup tent with which to conceal Heygirl. He cut out the floor using a sharp pair of scissors (the triplets had begged to help) and then put the top part of the tent over Heygirl. Her leash poked out from under the tent itself and her tail stuck out the door, but Spider hoped that even if the children were spotted, these little details would escape notice in the darkness.

"There now," Spider said, "between the pup tent and the picnic basket, we look like any other family planning a little oceanside cookout."

Except that it was two in the morning, they were

headed *away* from the beach, and the triplets were carrying a canister of liquid nitrogen hooked up to a weed sprayer.

When they got to the bottom of the hill, the freeze machine was transferred from the arms of Brick to the arms of Spike.

"In three blocks you'd better hand it over to me," Sassy demanded.

The children crept past the darkened houses that lined the streets of Eel-Smack-by-the-Bay. Their progress was slow; after all, the offspring of Endangered Albino Alligators are not the speediest animals on the close-to-extinction list . . . and Heygirl was further impeded by the pup tent. Spider held her leash in one hand and in his other a pork chop. Every so often he would wave the chop around on the other side of the tent from her snout to keep her going.

Spider took care to walk as close to low-growing hedges and shrubbery as possible in order to make the pup tent less visible.

When the children had traveled what Sassy

estimated to be the distance, she made a grab for the freeze machine. Spike refused to let go. "We haven't gone three blocks yet!" he whispered.

"Give"–tug–"it"–tug–"here!" Sassy screamed in a whisper, being Up to No Good. This is one advantage of the fact that the triplets whisper when they are Up to No Good. They are not frequent bickerers, but when they do fight, at least it's quiet.

"It *has* been three blocks! It's *my* turn!" She quit tugging and instead pushed Spike down. He landed on the sidewalk with a bump.

"Whadja do that for?!" Brick exclaimed in what he fondly imagined to be gangster speech and defended Spike by pushing Sassy down. She wasted no time in grabbing his ankles and yanking them toward her. Brick fell on top of Spike, who showed his objection to being landed upon by head-butting his brother. Soon the three were rolling around, punching, and biting one another with their sharp little teeth whenever a shin or a forearm presented itself to the biter. When that happened, the bitee would howl (very quietly) and turn on his or her attacker . . .

leaving him- or herself open to attack by the remaining triplet. It is a good thing that the three seldom resorted to this sort of physical conflict, or the Bellweather family's medical bills might have been very high.

Spider sighed and backed the tent up so that the opening flap was against a low-growing hedge. Family policy was to let any fight of the triplets run its course, since interference was likely to cause more than a little discomfort to the person intervening.

The sight of the triplets brawling *is* a distracting one, and Ninda and Spider were soon absorbed by the altercation.

"What's this about, then?" came the sound of a voice sharper than the triplets' teeth. Spider jumped and they stopped their scuffle immediately. The young animal conservationist spun around to see the pith-helmeted silhouette of his nemesis, Thaddeus Bohack.

"Just a family matter, sir. We're on our way home," Spider said, trying to sound casual. He stepped forward toward Bohack, dropping Heygirl's leash behind him as he did so. He didn't look down to see it snake out of sight.

"At two A.M.?" Bohack asked.

"We were out stargazing, sir," Spider said quickly, before any of the others could offer different explanations. "Mars is very bright tonight," he said.

"Indeed," said Bohack, not bothering to look up at the sky. "Just out for a stroll at two A.M., stargazing. . . ." His voice trailed off as his eyes came to rest on the container which held the hatchlings. "What's in the basket?"

"Gator tots!" Spike spoke up.

Sassy and Brick nudged one another, grinning at Spike's brilliance, and the battle of the freeze machine was forgotten forever.

"Just a midnight snack, sir. Tater tots," Spider spoke politely, hoping the dogcatcher hadn't heard Spike properly.

"Mmm," Bohack grunted. "And the tent?"

"In case the triplets got tired. They're awfully young to be up so late," Ninda said, sounding very adult.

"Then you won't mind if I have a look inside." The

dogcatcher strode over to the tent and tipped it up before anyone could stop him.

It is hard to say who was more surprised, Bohack or the children.

"There's nothing in here!" he said.

"There's nothing in there," the children repeated.

Heygirl was gone.

"See? Nothing here," Spider croaked.

The Animal Control officer looked around, suspicion in his eyes. He shook a finger at Spider.

"There may have been nothing here this time, young man, but I'm watching you!"

"Yes, sir." Spider was the very picture of calm, though his heart was pounding and he felt short of breath. Where could she be?

"We were just heading home, sir. Is that all right, sir?" Spider asked. The triplets gave theatrical yawns.

The dogcatcher briefly considered escorting the children home. Not to make sure they arrived there safely, of course, but to make sure they weren't Up to No Good. Fortunately for Spider, Thaddeus Bohack had been on the receiving end of Dr. Bellweather's sense of humor one too many times, and he was not anxious to greet the professor at two A.M.

"Well, go on then," he said with a snarl that would have done a vicious Chihuahua proud. "But remember, you're being watched, Spider Bellweather!"

"Yes, sir. I'll remember that, sir." Spider grabbed the tent and shooed the other children back in the direction from which they had come. He knew, without having to look, that Bohack watched them until they turned the corner.

"She must have gone through a hole in the hedge," Spider told his siblings in a low voice. "We need to double back behind the houses and try to find her."

The children spread out across moonlit backyards, peering at the shadowy places underneath low tree branches and looking into swimming pools. They didn't dare call out since they had no way of knowing whether Thaddeus Bohack had left the area.

Ninda's progress was slowed by the picnic basket and Sassy's by the freeze machine. Still, they checked doghouses and crept past patios. The entire group quickened their pace when they heard an insistent yipping coming from the vicinity of the mayor's huge, white house.

On one side of a wrought-iron fence yipped the mayoral poodle. On the other side, still wearing the leash, Heygirl strained to get into the yard. Spider was relieved to see that she was only able to fit about one third of her snout through the bars. Even so, she snapped her teeth and moved her tail from side to side and was a *very* menacing sight. The poodle yapped at her from the relative safety of the veranda.

"Heygirl, come," Spider commanded. The great beast ignored him. A light appeared in one of the upstairs windows. He tugged on the leash. "Come, now!" he insisted. If Bohack was in the area he'd surely come to see what all the barking was about. In desperation Spider seized the picnic basket from Ninda, grabbed one of the babies, and waved it wildly within the gator's line of sight. Thus reminded of her maternal duty, Heygirl abandoned her plans for Poodle Casserole and reluctantly pulled her snout free of the fence. The baby alligator didn't like being handled in such a manner and expressed her feelings by nipping at Spider. Heygirl looked on placidly while he hastily replaced the baby in its carrier.

The group beat a (relatively) hasty path down the last block to Our Lady of the Benevolent Soup. Once there they had no trouble gaining access to the church. Spider used the same method that he figured the collection-plate burglars used.

Along the back wall of the church was a grate very near the ground. This grate opened to a chute that in the old days had been used to slide coal down to the furnace room in the basement. The church now had electric heating, and the chute was no longer in use. Except by collection-plate thieves and alligator-bearing children, that is.

Once inside the basement, Spider directed the triplets to the places that the pipes should be frozen, while he and Ninda made Heygirl and her offspring comfortable.

When the triplets had used up all of the liquid nitrogen in the tank, they returned to Spider and

Ninda. They all spent a few more minutes cuddling the beasts. The children were sorry to leave, as they had become quite attached to the alligators.

Spider took a moment to savor the feeling of accomplishment that comes naturally to one who has realized his goal of establishing the first ever Endangered Albino Alligator Habitat. And to think, he'd managed to do it without being sent to the St. Whiplash Academy for Wayward Boys. Now that the animals were no longer in his possession, there wasn't much Thaddeus Bohack could do to him.

This time.

Best of all, Spider was sure Benway would be far more likely to stay now that he didn't have to fear physical harm.

"Here you are, Heygirl," Spider said, rubbing her head. "I'll slide food through the coal chute every day, and I'll come down those steps myself to check on you often." He pointed to them. He knew she didn't understand every word he said. She seemed to get the gist of it, though, because she settled down with the babies, right at the bottom of the stairs that led up to the church offices, the better to greet Spider when he should come to call.

———><———

August 26,
GLOAT minus 6 days, 4 hours, and 3 minutes

Dear Journal,

The children quite surprised me yesterday. Rather than leave the mop-up of Ninda's room to their most humble servant, they all pitched in to help. Perhaps such a gesture coming from Ninda was not so surprising, but the triplets???!!! I hardly knew how to respond.

I fear I <u>am</u> allergic to smoke, though. During the task my eyes watered quite a bit, and I had to leave the room. In my quarters, I reflected that had the children made such a gesture before, I might not have been Quite So Hasty in making the oath I did to leave them. Not that I would have stayed, or that I'm not Quite Glad to be

going—not at all. I just might not have been . . .
So Hasty. That's all.

Spider seems to have found a home for Heygirl and her babies sometime during the night. I
could review the videotapes to find out where
he took them. I have learned over the years,
however, not to concern myself with question-
ing small details as long as the outcome is desir-
able. The alligators are not <u>here</u>, and that is the
important thing. Smithers will no doubt waste a
lot of time before he learns to take that stance. If
he lasts more than a day, that is. "Keep your hands
where you can see them and lock your door"
indeed! At any rate, I expect I'll find out what
happened to Heygirl and the babies all too soon.
Of course, none of this will be of any concern to
me in 6 days, 4 hours, and 1 minute. Oh dear, my
smoke allergy is acting up. Must cease writing.

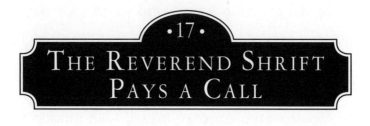

·17·
THE REVEREND SHRIFT
PAYS A CALL

When the Reverend Shrift returned from his "rest cure" up the coast, he must have tried to turn on a faucet in the vestry and discovered that no water would come out. He must have tried to get into the basement to see what the trouble with the pipes was. He must have discovered in a startling fashion that the basement was flooded and that there were now Endangered Albino Alligators living there. He must have realized immediately who was responsible.

"Bellweather!" the Reverend Shrift shouted, pounding on the door of the lighthouse. "Bellweather!" he shouted again, leaning on the doorbell. This was an unfortunate mistake, especially for a nervous person such as he.

Up close, the sudden blare hit with a deafening noise that sent shock waves through the body of the Reverend Shrift. He was propelled backward off the porch. Any calming effects of the "rest cure," had there been any, were utterly destroyed. The morning so far had proved too much for him. He sank down into a black-robed heap and did not rise when Lillian came to see who was at the door.

"Well hello, Reverend," she said. "What a treat to see you here!" She came out onto the lawn and sat down beside him. Lillian was incapable of true surprise. If the minister came to call and chose to have a seat on the front lawn, well, that was of small consequence to her.

"How are things at church?" she asked conversationally, tucking her feet underneath her and smoothing her paint-speckled skirt.

The Reverend Shrift whimpered.

"Pardon?" she asked.

"Ogillatores in the bosment," was the Reverend Shrift's gibbering response.

"Ogilwho?" Lillian asked.

"Aglliators in the besmont," he flustered.

"You seem a little excited, Reverend." Lillian patted his hand. "How about some nice chamomile tea? Or"—she leaned conspiratorially toward him—"it's early yet, but I think I have some lovely elderberry wine."

She called for Benway to please bring refreshments out to the lawn.

Spider had come upstairs when the foghorn sounded. He crouched underneath an open window that faced the front lawn.

When Benway brought refreshments, Lillian pressed a little glass into the Reverend's trembling hand. "Shhh," she hushed him when he would have spoken. "Drink up first, and then you can tell me what's on your mind."

The Reverend finished the contents of his glass in a gulp, and then held it out to be refilled with a much steadied hand. Lillian obliged him.

"Now then," she said. "What's this about ogil . . . ?"

"Alligators in the basement," the Reverend Shrift finally managed to get out.

"Oh! How splendid." Lillian smiled. "I can see why you're so excited. We have alligators in our basement as well. Of course, ours are Endangered Albino Alligators," she said with pride. "Very rare you know, but I'm sure yours must be just as lovely."

"Mrs. Bellweather," the Reverend began.

"Oh, please call me Lillian," she said. "I'm so glad you came to visit. You know, my son Spider is a bit of an expert when it comes to reptiles. Perhaps he could give you a hand with yours."

Spider chose this moment to scramble through the open window. The Reverend Shrift's anxiety had given him a brilliant idea for dealing with the mess at hand.

"Actually, Mother, those are my alligators," he said. "Heygirl and the hatchlings."

"Oh, how nice!" Lillian exclaimed. She turned to the Reverend. "What a wonderful place for them. They *are* dear, but we were getting a little crowded here. Also, Benway seemed to be a tiny bit nervous around them. All that snapping and so forth."

The Reverend Shrift gave a start at the word *snapping.* "They cannot stay," he said. His voice rose to a panicky pitch. "I c-c-can't have ogillators in the bosment of my church."

"Oh, dear," said Mrs. Bellweather. "Is there something in the Bible about that?"

"I don't think so, Mother, I think he just doesn't want them," Spider said.

"Exactly," gasped the Reverend Shrift gratefully.

"He'd rather deal with burglars, possibly armed and dangerous burglars, face-to-face," Spider said.

"I'm glad you understand, young man, I . . . *what?*" shouted the Reverend when the impact of Spider's words hit him.

"Oh, I think it's terribly brave of you," Spider said. "Imagine making the choice to risk a dangerous confrontation with criminals, rather than rely on the protection that a basement full of Endangered Albino Alligators could give you." He leaned over. "May I shake your hand, sir? I am proud to know such a courageous soul." Spider shook the Reverend's limp hand, and then turned to his mother. "After all," he explained, "the alligators would have posed no risk to him, confined to the basement as they are, or would have been. However, they would have kept burglars from entering the church." Spider shook his head, as if amazed. "Why, I'll bet that just the publicity that the first ever Endangered Albino Alligator Habitat was on the premises would have kept thieves from even *thinking* of breaking and entering." Spider patted the Reverend on the shoulder. "And there you are, choosing not to take advantage of the dumb beasts, but rather to risk engagement in hand-to-hand combat with evildoing criminals. You are a brave man indeed!" he told the shuddering Reverend.

"I think the church basement is a *lovely* place for Heygirl to raise her hatchlings." Lillian poured yet another glass of elderberry wine for the minister, smiling the sweet smile of someone with whom others never, ever argue.

August 28,
GLOAT minus 4 days, 2 hours, and 7 minutes

Dear Journal,

The Reverend Shrift has agreed to allow Hey-girl and the hatchlings to stay in the basement of Our Lady of the Benevolent Soup. Imagine this, Dear Journal—Spider has actually proposed to name the preserve after me! It is to be called the Tristan Benway Endangered Albino Alligator Habitat.

I must see about getting some allergy shots. Recently I am finding that my eyes water entirely too much.

At any rate, thanks be to Spider (and Mrs. Bellweather, of course), I am certain that the Reverend Shrift's collection plates shall never be robbed again. Even so, that knowledge seems not to have eased his mind or his nerves. If ever a man needed to develop a stiff upper lip, it would be that chap, there. I am in favor of an immersion therapy of sorts. Perhaps he should spend a week with the Bellweathers. I daresay he shan't understand them any better than I do (after all, there's no understanding chaos); nevertheless, I must say, that after years of employment with this family, I am a man possessed of nerves of steel. Who knew that there could be any benefit to me in my association with Bellweathers? That is certainly something to ponder.

In other exciting matters, I held in my hands the first copy of my book today. The title is <u>Life Among the Savages of the Lighthouse</u> but in my heart it is F-R-E-E-D-O-M!" I shall pack my bags tonight, as I will most assuredly have to leave Eel-Smack-by-the-Bay soon, and with haste.

Upon leafing through it, though, I couldn't help noticing that while the events recounted in the manuscript are factual, they do paint a very grim picture of the family I have served in my loyal, faithful, and hardworking fashion. This has never concerned me before . . . but knowing that Spider and Ninda will inevitably read what

I have written about them, I confess myself to be a trifle uncomfortable.

I am hopeful that they have no idea about the reading and book-signing party. I wonder if it is too late to ask Isbn to remove the advertisement from the window of his bookstore. After all, my time with the Bellweathers is soon to be at an end. I should not like to have them think ill of me when I've gone. Not that what they think of me <u>really</u> matters. I simply believe it unprofessional to hurt the feelings of one's employers. That is all.

·18·
A Dis-Alarming Task

Eel-Smack-by-the-Bay is not a particularly large village, and the good citizens who wished to view the *Mona Lisa* did so in the first couple of days. The crowd at the museum thinned out considerably after that.

A few days into the painting's exhibition, the triplets made their move. At forty minutes to closing time, armed with a heavy magnet, they stood outside the door marked AUTHORIZED PERSONNEL ONLY.

"I'm authorized to take out the trash at home," Spike whispered.

"Good enough for me," Sassy told him.

Brick pushed through the door and they found themselves in a brightly lit office. There were several television monitors along one wall; these were hooked up to security cameras that were trained on different parts of the museum. There was a desk in front of the screens. On this desk sat the computer. In front of it sat the Walrus. He was playing with the cap to his uniform, tossing it into the air and catching it. When he noticed the triplets standing in the doorway he yelled at them.

"What are you doing? You're not supposed to be in here!"

Sassy burst in to tears. Loudly, although she was Up to No Good.

"I THOUGHT THIS WAS THE BATHROOM!" she wailed.

The big man looked panicked. "Oh, honey, there, there," he tried to soothe her over her shrieking sobs.

"WAAAAAAAH!" Sassy screamed, enjoying herself thoroughly.

"YOU'RE SCARING HER," yelled Brick. Though

he, too, was Up to No Good, he had to yell in order to be heard over his sister's shrieking.

"I didn't mean to scare you," the watchman said. Sassy continued to wail.

"I'll show you to the bathroom. Take my hankie." The Walrus fished his handkerchief from his pocket and offered it to Sassy, who quieted down and dabbed at her eyes. While the Walrus's attention was focused on Sassy, Spike slipped the heavy magnet out of the back of his pocket and sneakily attached it to the computer's hard drive. The screen went momentarily fuzzy, and then cleared. The alarm system was disabled.

"Thank you for the handkerchief." Sassy continued to dab her eyes, making sure the guard's attention was still on her.

"The bathroom is just down this hall," he told her, opening the office door. Brick nudged the thermostat up.

The Walrus, Spike, and Brick waited for Sassy outside the restroom. Spike and Brick peppered Walrus with questions. Did he get to carry a gun? How many cavemen could be eaten by a stuffed tiger? How loud was the Big Bang?

Sassy stood on the sink and opened the bathroom window, which was just the right size for a medium-ish painting to slip through. Then she came out of the bathroom and thanked Walrus, just as they heard Whippet call out, "Thirty minutes to closing time." The triplets thanked Walrus in their prettiest way and walked in the direction of the museum entrance. As soon as they heard the office door close behind him, they scampered over to hide in the natural-history exhibit.

———

August 30,
OAT (while it is Oath Abandonment Time, in truth I can no longer consider the Liberation strictly Glorious) minus 1 day, 22 hours, and 14 minutes

Dear Journal,
It would seem that the triplets are cultivating

a fine taste for culture; they've apparently been spending quite a bit of time at the Eel-Smack museum. A whole wad of museum-entry tickets fell out of Spike's pockets last night. I do not know, nor will I ever understand how it is that three individuals who've done nothing all their lives but destroy can take an interest in something as sublime and benign (if created using the usual methods) as Art. I've no idea what they may be up to; however, I will admit to a certain satisfaction in knowing that the Light-house on the Hill is safe from their destruction for a change.

I must confess that I continue to have mis-givings about my book-writing venture. Isbn has declined to remove the notice in the window of his bookstore, as he says it has generated a lot of interest and is Good for Business.

Events have been set in motion, and it's no use crying over spilled milk. However, I do have the comfort of knowing that at least my version of events is fair and honest.

Should Smithers (the sure-to-be-disloyal prat) ever choose to write a similar chronicle of the family (there will continue to be a wealth of material there, I'm afraid), it will no doubt contain inaccuracies and slurs.

·19·
THE TRIPLETS STEAL THE *MONA LISA*

"I'm already too hot," Spike complained, whispering of course. The three were crouched in front of the Styrofoam cave. They had donned their panther costumes from Halloween and joined the exhibit at a moment when no one was looking. This wasn't difficult to do. It was so close to closing time that most of the visitors were in the gift shop except for a small boy, tugging at his mother, who pushed a stroller with a very ugly baby in it.

Eventually the doors to the museum were shut and locked, and Whippet went home. The triplets settled in. They felt it best to wait until darkness fell to make off with the painting.

"After all," Spike said, "it wouldn't do at all to parade *Mona Lisa* through the streets."

"And doing it in the light of day might take away some of the anonymity we were hoping to achieve," said Brick.

They passed the time in between Walrus's hourly walking checks of the museum by reading from a book of natural disasters and talking over the ones they liked best.

The 1815 eruption of Mount Tambora was a great favorite. It was the largest volcanic eruption in recorded history. The messy aftermath of tons of cubic kilometers of material was an added bonus to the disaster.

"I wonder how Benway'd like to clean that up?" Brick asked Spike and Sassy.

For sheer disaster magnitude, though, the tri-state tornado of 1925, which left a 219-mile track and raged over Missouri, Illinois, and Indiana, got the vote of the triplets. They spent a pleasant, if warm, time in discussion.

"Why's it have to be so hot?" complained Spike.

"I turned up the thermostat 'cause I was hoping Walrus'd get drowsy and not come around so often," Brick explained.

His idea seemed to work. The next two hours passed without a visit from Walrus, and the triplets decided it was time to act.

Still garbed in their panther costumes, the three made their way out of the natural-history wing and down the corridor to the fine-art wing. Spike carried the canister with their masterpiece in it, and one of the quilts. Brick carried the other quilt, two pillow-cases, and the flashlight. Sassy carried the grappling hooks, for she hadn't given up the hope that they would come in handy.

They made their way back to the fine-art wing. The *Mona Lisa* waited for them, smiling coyly (or so they imagined) from her place on the wall behind a red velvet rope. Once again the triplets were enchanted.

"That is a very Grand and Fine-Looking red velvet rope," Spike whispered to Sassy and Brick.

"Imagine the uses to which a Grand and Fine-

Looking red velvet rope could be put," whispered Sassy back.

"It's clear that we should give Benway this very Grand and Fine-Looking red velvet rope, as well as the painting," Brick whispered, then added, "Maybe he'll let us borrow it sometimes."

The *Mona Lisa* isn't huge (approximately thirty inches by twenty). It's painted on a panel rather than on canvas, and this coupled with its ornate frame makes it rather heavy. The triplets managed to get it down off the wall, stuffed into two pillowcases, one at either end, and wrapped into two quilts. The children leaned the bundle against the wall and went about the business of hanging their masterpiece. Despite their admiration for da Vinci's art, they still considered THEIR painting to be the superior work, and had not lost sight of the original purpose of their little escapade.

They were disconcerted, however, to realize that they had neglected to bring anything with which to hang their masterpiece.

"*You* were supposed to bring the hammer and nails," Sassy whispered to Brick.

"No, *you* were," Brick whispered back.

"No, *you* were," Spike whispered to them both.

Brick had a scathingly brilliant idea and the three finally crept to the gift shop, where they cleaned out the display of chewing gum.

"We'll not be able to put this back after anonymously borrowing it," Spike said.

"But at least it won't be leaving the museum," Brick pointed out.

The three sat next to one of the most valuable paintings in the world, their mouths full of sticky goo.

"Mmmmff, groouble romph?" Sassy asked. (How much do you think is enough?)

"Drmms, mmmfffpp," Brick said. (Oh, four or five packs, I suppose.)

As soon as the gobs in their mouths became nice and stickily juicy, they took them out and popped in fresh pieces.

"Grrbble, whmph hrmmml mhhhdp," said Spike. (On second thought, I believe my favorite disaster is the Mount Tambora explosion.)

Once they'd amassed enough of the sticky mess to

adhere their art to the wall, they took their painting out of the canister in which it had been stored. Sassy and Brick unrolled it while Spike shined the flashlight over it.

"Truly magnificent," Sassy sighed.

"Pure genius," Spike agreed.

"Brilliant," Brick said.

They weren't quite tall enough to hang the work at eye level, so Brick balanced on Sassy's shoulders and Spike passed the painting up to him. Brick pounded the lumps of gum flat to the wall and placed the canvas over them.

"*Sssshhh,*" Sassy whispered.

"I don't want a lumpy canvas," Brick hissed down to her, pounding the surface of the canvas to the wall now.

"I thought I heard something," Sassy said. Brick stopped pounding.

The sound of clomping security-guard feet could be heard in the corridor. Walrus had woken up.

Brick jumped down from Sassy's shoulders. He landed on the tile floor with a soft, "Ouch."

Heavy footsteps paused just outside the open door. The triplets exchanged anxious glances, held their breath, and tried to come up with plausible excuses for why they were in the museum at all—and more importantly, why the *Mona Lisa* was bundled up like a two-year-old on the first snowy day of the year. Just when they thought they'd pass out from holding their breath, the night watchman moved on. They didn't relax until they heard the sound of the office door closing from down the hallway.

"Walrus should be fired. He didn't even look in here," Sassy whispered.

"Imagine not checking out the room with the *Mona Lisa* in it," Brick said.

"Just suppose there were criminals in here instead of us?" Spike whispered.

They gave the security guard twenty minutes or so to settle in, then prepared to leave.

Spike carried the swaddled *Mona Lisa*, while Sassy and Brick each picked up one of the heavy posts that were attached to the Very Fine-Looking red velvet rope. The little procession had to stop a number of times so that Sassy and Brick could get a better handle on their load. Though the triplets considered themselves remarkably strong, each step was hesitant due to the heaviness of their burden, and the journey down the dark corridor was a long one.

"You first," Sassy whispered to Spike when they stood outside the restroom door. He just stood there, holding the bundled-up *Mona Lisa*.

"It's a girls' bathroom. You go first," Spike said.

Sassy set down her pole and took the painting from Spike. She went into the bathroom, and there was a thunderous clunk out in the hallway. Spike had underestimated the weight of the pole that was attached to the Very Fine-Looking red velvet rope and dropped it. From far down the corridor they heard Walrus's door slam open.

Sassy propped the painting against a toilet, then scrambled onto the sink. She looked out the window and realized she was some distance from the ground. Spike and Brick burst into the bathroom tugging the lovely velvet rope, which dragged the two heavy poles in a loud and clanging manner before tearing loose. All attempts at stealth were abandoned.

They could hear Walrus running down the hall.

"I take back what I said about firing him," Sassy gasped. It was a long way down to the ground. "We'll have to jump with the painting," Brick said.

"It might get broken," Sassy objected.

Wheezing footsteps clomped nearer. The three looked down. "It sure is a long way to the ground," Brick observed.

"I'm not jumping."

"Me neither."

Sassy held up the grappling hooks. "We don't have to," she said, quickly attaching them to the ends of the very Grand and Fine-Looking red velvet rope. She hooked the rope to a pipe underneath the sink and threw it (the rope, not the sink) out the window.

"*Voilà*," she said. She was smug. "We can climb down."

"How are we going to get the painting down?" Spike asked.

Brick poked his head out the window and saw a

familiar figure skulking in the shadows. He was so grateful that he didn't stop to wonder why on earth *that* particular person should be hanging around the museum in the dead of night.

"The only way," he said. "The Benway."

They pushed the painting through the window and practically on top of their very surprised butler.

"This is for you! Run!" Sassy hissed. After the briefest hesitation, Benway did so.

The panther suit–clad figures rappelled down the very Grand and Fine-Looking red velvet rope. On the ground, after tugging it free, the three ran in the opposite direction Benway had taken. A half block from the museum they collided with none other than Thaddeus Bohack, who was just coming around the corner. The Animal Control officer was knocked to the ground. Spike snarled at him in a most terrifying way and the three ran on. The man who usually caught dogs spent a few moments trying to catch his breath. By the time he did, the triplets were long gone, and the night watchman was leaning out of the window and shouting.

August 31,
Liberation of Oath and going on my Way (LOW)
minus 58 minutes

Dear Journal,

I've just had the most extraordinary evening
of my life. I went to check up on the triplets,
something Smithers is sure never to do. The
three did not return to the Lighthouse on the
Hill after supper and I knew they were either Up
to No Good, or (and I admit this is a new thought
for me) somehow in trouble. I went round to
the museum, for I had deduced in my clever
way that whatever mischief they were planning
would be centered upon the location of their
frequent visits. I was not prepared, however, for
the magnitude of the mischief they had gotten up
to this time. They threw a largish, quilt-covered
object at me and told me to run. I am not accustomed to taking orders from the junior members

of the household, but it did occur to me that I had just become an accomplice to some criminal activity or other and that if I did not do as bid immediately, there were sure to be uncomfortable consequences in the event of my capture.

Imagine my astonishment upon unwrapping this Particular Object in the privacy of my boudoir. It took me a thunderously long moment to grasp the fact that I, Tristan Benway, actually held in my mortal hands da Vinci's masterpiece, the <u>Mona Lisa</u>.

Oh, the things that went through my head. I gazed upon it, struck with awe at both the fine work <u>and</u> the extreme audacity of the crime. Even for the triplets, this really was going too far. Somewhere, it dimly occurred to me that I ought to notify the Authorities. . . . And yet . . . and yet . . . there I stood, holding in my possession arguably the most famous work of art in the civilized world. (I cannot attest to what the most famous work of art in the uncivilized world might be.)

The triplets had stolen it for <u>me</u>! I gently touched my fingers to that famous smile. . . . Certainly I am one of the only people in history to have had opportunity to do such a thing. A queer kind of thrill went through my soul as I did so . . . quite similar, I fancy, to the thrills that the Bellweathers must often experience during their escapades. Cut-up suit art, dangerous beasts, protests, and bagpipe playing must all result in like feeling. Should such stimulation become commonplace to me, there would undoubtedly be damage to my nervous system and heart. I am not so sprightly as I once was; however, I do feel lighter now and . . . younger somehow. . . . Perhaps a once-in-a-while thrill wouldn't be such a harmful thing. . . .

I believe I am close to understanding this family, of comprehending what motivates them to behave as they do. This sudden and newfound insight subdues me into a shocked wonder. Might they truly be the geniuses they are always claiming to be?

The triplets came into my room a quarter of an hour later. They were dressed in their Halloween costumes—an odd choice considering that holiday's nearly two months away. Of course I advised them to return the masterpiece immediately.

"But it's for you," Brick whispered.

"We wanted to give you something Grand and Fine," whispered Sassy.

"So you'd stay," Spike whispered.

I truly do not know which is the more surprising thing: that the triplets managed to steal the <u>Mona Lisa</u>, or that their motive in doing so was to get <u>me</u> to stay on. I had been so certain that when I left, these three, out of everyone in the family, would take no notice of the fact that someone else occupied my position.

I thought of the bananas and gravy I had been careful to include in this evening's menu. I do not understand the triplets' tastes, but as a Great Servant I have always taken care to provide them with what would make them happiest. . . . Is it possible that my efforts have not gone unnoticed?

Fishing a hankie from my bedside table, I chose to address neither this, nor the question of how they knew of my plans to leave. Instead I engaged them in an informative discussion dealing with the penalties for Grand Theft.

"You must certainly return the masterpiece," I finally concluded.

Sassy had a rather sly look on her face. "Would you stay then?" she asked.

"I will consider it," I told her, though I had no intention of doing so. I must confess that it gave my conscience a twinge. I had vowed to leave, and leave I must; yet here was I, a Benway, dishonorably implying something different. And to a child in my care, no less!

Still, they must certainly return the masterpiece. If this is the only way to get them to do so, then . . . I've no doubt they will find a unique way to accomplish it. I can only hope that my involvement in the theft will never come to light.

Oh, I hope that dunderheaded fool Smithers will have at least intelligence enough to appreciate them. Of course, he shall never know this family as I have, and he will certainly be the poorer for that. (I can scarcely believe I penned that last sentence. . . .)

The celebration of my book at Isbn's Book Shoppe is to take place in 12 hours . . . and by tomorrow night I shall be Far, Far Away, the terms of my Hasty Oath fulfilled and my bond to this family broken forever.

·20·
WRAPPING IT UP

The triplets stood in Benway's quarters, admiring the painting, which they'd hung (with some difficulty due to its weight), on the back of the door.

"I wonder how it'd look if we touched it up a bit," Sassy whispered.

"What if we painted a stick of dynamite into the background?" Brick wondered quietly, since he was Up to No Good.

"Do you think the paint will have a chance to dry before we wrap it up to take it back?" Spike whispered.

Benway had managed to convince them that as

much as he appreciated the gift, the painting needed to be returned to the museum in order for him to stay. He had also managed to impress upon them the fact that their beloved acts of arson and mayhem would be curtailed in prison.

"Imagine, wanting to lock up little children, just for giving someone a present!" The three were indignant but convinced. More so when they read of the hulla-baloo surrounding their escapade in the morning edition of the paper.

THE LADY DISAPPEARS!!! the newspaper head-line screamed.

Local police were summoned to the Eel-Smack museum early this morning following an inco-herent telephone call from the museum's night watchman. Federal authorities were called in once it was evident from his gibberish that da Vinci's masterpiece, the *Mona Lisa*, had disappeared.

Reaction from the French has been scathing.

"I knew it was a mistake to loan a treasure such as the *Mona Lisa* to a people who cannot pronounce frappé correctly," fumed the president of France. "These cretins are responsible for what is truly an INTERNATIONAL INCIDENT!"

Inexplicably both the night watchman and the local Animal Control officer, who was on the scene at the time of the crime, believe the precious work of art was stolen by a pack of large black cats. Police will neither confirm nor deny reports that the two have been removed to the Shady Acres Spa and Sanatorium for a "rest cure."

"Certainly being responsible for the loss of the most famous work of art in the world would unhinge a weak mind," said an anonymous museum spokesperson. "As for that Bohack fellow, well, he always was a bit of a nutter."

A work of art was left in place of the famous painting. (See related story, page 17A.)

The triplets nearly ripped the newspaper apart turning to page 17A.

The headline on that page read, *Replacement Work Not Without Merit,* according to area critic.

"WHAT ABOUT BRILLIANT?" Brick screamed.

"The painting left in place of the *Mona Lisa* is experimental in the extreme," says Harlan Snodgrass, Eel-Smack-by-the Bay's premier critic. "It combines all of the landscapes you've ever seen in your life with amazingly realistic portraits and the most whimsical abstract art. While I do not condone the theft of the *Mona Lisa*, I must say that the creator of the piece left in substitute shows promise." Museum officials have no immediate plans to remove the painting. Visitors may view it during regular hours.

"JUST PROMISE?" shrieked Sassy.

"DOESN'T THE MAN APPRECIATE GENIUS WHEN HE SEES IT?" yelled Brick.

"Someday Mr. Harlan Snodgrass is going to be taught a little lesson about criticizing *our* art," whispered Spike.

Various schemes for returning the *Mona Lisa* directly to the museum were considered and rejected.

The triplets enjoyed the thought of returning the work of art in a spectacular way, perhaps involving smoke and an explosion of some sort, but soon realized that such a plan might somehow harm their painting.

"I find myself becoming a fan of the more subdued approach," Sassy whispered. Her siblings agreed with her.

"Isn't it funny that it's so much easier to anonymously borrow something than it is to abandon it?" Spike wondered.

"It is," Brick agreed. "Except, remember that movie we saw where the mother couldn't take care of her baby so she left it on the steps of the church to be found? She didn't get caught."

"Imagine how easy it would be to abandon something on the steps of Short Shrift's church." Sassy was excited. And so the triplets plan for the safe return of the *Mona Lisa* was hatched.

That afternoon, the Reverend Shrift discovered a huge basket on the front steps of Our Lady of the

Benevolent Soup. His joy at discovering that there was no baby in the basket (he was very afraid of babies, loud creatures that they are), was tempered by the shocking discovery of what the basket truly contained. He was sitting on the steps of the church still clutching the *Mona Lisa* and blathering senselessly when his secretary came back from lunch. First she called the authorities to come pick up the painting. Then she called Shady Acres Spa and Sanitarium. The person who took the call wondered if there would soon be anyone left in Eel-Smack-by-the-Bay, as the sanitarium seemed to be filling up with citizens from that village.

It was with the sense of a job well done that the triplets joined Spider and Ninda, who were on their way to Isbn's Book Shoppe. The store was very crowded by the time they arrived. Eel-Smack-by-the-Bay, for all of its charms, had never had the distinction of an author in its midst. Some people such as Postman Grimsby showed up to see if the book held incriminating details that would aid in pressing charges against the family. Nearly as many people showed up to hear Benway read at the party as had shown up to view the *Mona Lisa*.

Copies of the memoir were stacked on shelves near the front door. The rumbling hum of expectation among the crowd was punctuated by the lucrative *cha-ching* of the store's cash register as it rang up purchases of the book. Eli Isbn himself hustled around trying to get people to shut up so that he could introduce Benway. Finally, he went over to the table where the new author was seated, signing copies. He turned on a microphone and banged it against a stack of the books. The amplified noise was so deafening that it shut everyone up in a hurry—everyone except the triplets, of course.

"STUPENDOUS!" Sassy screamed.

"DO IT AGAIN!" Spike shrieked.

"PLEASE?" Brick shouted, remembering his manners. Spider and Ninda shushed them.

Isbn glared into the crowd, but he couldn't see where the shouts had come from. He thanked everyone for coming and then turned the microphone over to Benway, who opened his book to a random chapter and, with much throat clearing, began to read. He seemed a bit nervous, and every once in a while he'd glance over at the children, gauging their reaction. They were transfixed.

"We're even more brilliant than I thought," Spike said to his siblings.

"Benway really gets us!" Sassy remarked.

"How in the world does he ALWAYS know what's going on?" Brick asked. "It's as if he has eyes in the back of his head!"

When Benway finished reading, there was a hush. Then into the silence came a thunderous applause. It was not entirely clear to Benway if people were applauding his skill as a writer, or simply his survival in the face of the Bellweather family chaos.

Whichever it was, there was such a din that the roar of Dr. Bellweather could barely be heard. He had caught wind of the reading but had not arrived in time to actually hear it.

The professor's eyebrows were wild, and words spewed forth from his mouth, words so terrible that it was a good thing the sound of the crowd drowned them out. He was trailed by Lillian, her face as serene as ever. The only thing that betrayed the haste with which she had followed her husband was the fact that she still clutched a paint brush. Ninda caught sight of her father shoving his way through the throng of people. Thinking fast, she grabbed Spider and they pushed their way toward their parents.

"When I get my hands on that . . . !" Dr. Bellweather shouted.

"Dad, did you just get here?" Ninda asked when they intercepted him.

"I did and I'm going to strangle that monkey-suited weasel!"

"Now, dear, his clothing comes from Tuxedos and Ice Cream. Hardly the sort of store which would cater to monkeys!" Lillian's musical voice was nearly lost in the crowd.

"You didn't hear Benway read?" Ninda asked.

"No, but I didn't need to! I told him I'd pulverize him if he ever, ever . . . !"

"Wrote a book on the care and maintenance of

lighthouses?" Ninda asked, nudging Spider. It wasn't a total lie, since Benway had devoted a chapter to the trials and tribulations of trying to keep the place looking presentable despite the best efforts of the triplets to destroy it from time to time.

The professor pushed his way closer to Benway, who looked alarmed.

Lillian laid her hand gently on her husband's arm. "Now, dear," she said, "we don't pulverize anyone, especially not family, and that's what Benway is." She smiled her sweet smile.

Dr. Bellweather didn't argue with her. No one ever does. Without looking again at Benway, he allowed himself to be towed back through the crowd.

Lillian looked back and called over her shoulder in her silvery voice, "We'll see you at home, Benway, dear." She paused for a moment, looking at his watery eyes with concern. "We'll get you some medicine for those allergies."

Dr. Bellweather only ever read scientific journals and newspapers. Lillian only ever read the backs of paint cans. If Ninda could get her parents away from the bookstore quickly, she was fairly certain they would never actually read Benway's book, or know its true subject matter. Certainly none of the villagers in Eel-Smack-by-the-Bay would dare broach the subject.

Dr. Bellweather's eyebrows were settling down. "Are you sure it's a book of household hints?" he asked.

"Perfectly." Ninda and Spider crossed their fingers behind their backs, as they nudged the professor out the door.

"It was actually kind of boring," Spider said.

"Now see? All your fuss for nothing." Lillian leaned up and kissed the tip of Dr. Bellweather's nose. Somehow she managed to leave a butter-yellow smear across his shirtfront as she did so.

"Really?" Dr. Bellweather asked, his eyebrows relaxing still more. He smiled down at his wife. "Imagine that! Well, well, well. Perhaps *I'll* write a book. Show him how it's done, eh?" The thought of one-upping Benway made the professor's eyebrows positively serene.

"What would your book be about, Dad?" Spider asked, leading both his parents back out the door of the book shop.

"Well, I think concrete would be a fascinating subject for a book. People would clamor to read all about the process of making it." Dr. Bellweather sounded sure.

As the four walked home he described the making of concrete in such boring detail that his eyebrows drowsed off to sleep. Ninda winked at Spider behind the professor's back. The danger was past.

———⊰●⊱———

September 1,

Dear Journal,

My life gets more and more strange. Today is September the first, and the fateful day of my book celebration. The children turned out to hear it. I was relieved that they seemed not to take any of the things I read out loud about them amiss. By some act of providence, the professor missed the actual reading. My skin is safe, for the time being.

I signed books for nearly two hours. I was quite gratified by the response to my humble effort. A rather tall chap I'd never before seen in Eel-Smack-by-the-Bay came up and handed me his business card. It said:

Lee Kubrickstan
Hollywood Director

He introduced himself to me and said he'd come to Eel-Smack-by-the-Bay because he'd read an advance copy of my book and wanted to talk to me. He thought my little tome might make a good movie. He was skeptical that it was non-fiction.

"Course you'll want to move out to where the action is. Make sure no one messes with the story too much. We'll get you all set up—before you know it, the studios will start a bidding war, and you'll be able to kick back and enjoy the rest of your life. People are gonna love this story." He said this all in the casual, yet expansive West Coast way one associates with Hollywood. . . .

Ahhh, Sunshine. A little cottage by the ocean. Drinks with umbrellas in them. Prize-winning plumerias. No stairs. A Life to call my Own.

These were my thought as I gazed at his business card.

And yet, somehow the notion of those things has lost a bit of its sheen.

Still, I pocketed the card, and told Kubrickstan that I would most certainly get back to him. I then returned to signing books.

When the crowd dwindled to almost nothing, the triplets approached me. They said not a word. They didn't shout and they didn't whisper. They wrapped their arms around me. We stood there for a moment, in perfect communion.

I thought of the business card in my pocket, and then of my cut-up suits.

I thought of hobos at the dinner table, and

then of Ninda's inquiry into whether I was feeling Downtrodden or Exploited.

I thought of Heygirl snapping and nipping at my toes, and then of Spider's new name for the Endangered Albino Alligator Habitat.

I thought of my ruined garden, and then of how it had felt to actually touch the <u>Mona Lisa</u>. I thought of the fact that the triplets had stolen it for <u>me</u>.

Finally, I thought of my quiet Cottage Far, Far Away, and I thought of Lillian Bellweather's startling and sweet words.

"Benway is family."

I've always had the notion that the Benways were my only family. I see now that I was Mistaken. I gazed down on the triplets' tousled, golden heads and knew that I wasn't going anywhere.

Hollywood will have to find another story, just as Wodehouse Smithers will have to find another family. I've found mine.

THE END

It is an Inescapable Truth that for most families, quiet would reign after such an extended period of Chaos and Activity. The Bellweathers, however, are not Most Families, and I can assure you that tranquility never lasts long with them. That is another story for another day, however.

ACKNOWLEDGMENTS AND DISCLAIMER

The acknowledgment page is supremely boring to read—unless, of course, an individual happens to be one of the people being acknowledged. Here's the tricky part—I may not remember to mention everyone I should, and I'll feel terrible if an individual, having every reason to suppose that he or she is **OF COURSE** going to be thanked by me in print, were to read the whole boring list and not find his or her name on it. To be on the safe side, no one who thinks they'll be thanked should read this. Just assume your name is here, because it should be. Okay?

As always it starts with family—I appreciate all of the Venutis for inspiring the Bellweathers, and especially Johnathon, Max, and Chelsea for being so delightful and amazing and lovable and talented, just like your dad. Giant thanks to my beloved Steve— I adore you more than I can say. Thanks, of course, to Tom and Jeanne Clark and also to Dave Weide the Science Guide. Deepest gratitude goes to two of my very favorite people in the universe, Kathleen Wolski and Kevin McCaughey. You walked every step of the way with me, even when it (and I) was tedious. I owe a huge debt to the Blue Rock Writers (and to Guillermo Alvarez, of course). Thanks to Kelly Sheahan for being an astute reader and an amazing individual! Ditto Ellen Bass. Thank you to my earliest readers, Carol Bierach, Audriana and Valerie Hull, Charlotte Sparacino, Sitar Terrass-Shah, and Claire and Ian-Thomas Shelton. MAJOR thanks are due to SCBWI and especially to Kim Turrisi—the matchmaker to the matchmaker. You had the wisdom and insight to recognize that Tracey Adams (equal parts favorite person and fabulous agent—thanks!) and I would be a great fit. My full heart thanks Susan Hart Lindquist—an awesome writer and an even more awesome human being—for taking me in at that first conference. I treasure you. And finally, thank you to all of the fun and fine folk at Egmont USA—but especially my Very Smart editor, Regina Griffin, and Very Eagle-Eyed copy editor, Nico Medina, and Very Responsible editorial assistant, Alison Weiss, not to mention Very Wacky (but oh, so brilliant) publisher, Elizabeth Law. You all inspire me.

KRISTIN CLARK VENUTI wrote on many things while growing up, including her father's prized dictionary, her mother's walls, and the family dog (with blueberry ink, of course). Now a children's-theater producer, scene painter, and two-time black belt, she lives with her husband, children, and their ink-free dog in the Santa Cruz Mountains of California. *Leaving the Bellweathers* is her first novel. You can visit her online at www.leavingthebellweathers.com.